Rayner
Heppenstall
A Critical Study

Library of Congress Cataloging-in-publication Data

Buckell, Gareth, 1981-
    Rayner Heppenstall / Gareth Buckell. -- 1st ed.
        p. cm.
    ISBN-13: 978-1-56478-471-1 (alk. paper)
    ISBN-10: 1-56478-471-1 (alk. paper)
    1. Heppenstall, Rayner, 1911---Criticism and interpretation. I. Title.
        PR6015.E56Z58 2007
        828'.91203--dc22
        [B]

                        2006035019

Partially funded by a grant from the Illinois Arts Council, a state agency, and by the
University of Illinois, Urbana-Champaign

Dalkey Archive Press is a nonprofit organization whose mission is to promote international
cultural understanding and provide a forum for dialogue for the literary arts

www.dalkeyarchive.com

Printed on permanent/durable acid-free paper, bound in the United States of
America, and distributed throughout North America and Europe

Rayner
Heppenstall
A Critical Study

G. J. Buckell

Champaign · London

Contents

Preface

Rayner Heppenstall was many things during his lifetime: a Catholic and an agnostic, a revolutionary and a reactionary, a pacifist and a soldier, a poet and a critic, a journalist and a broadcaster, a criminologist and a critic. However, he was a novelist above all, and if he is remembered for anything, it is his fiction.

However, in the early twenty-first century, it seems Heppenstall is not remembered, either for the numerous innovative programmes he produced for BBC Radio during its 'Golden Age' of the forties and fifties, or his novels. All that remains in print of Heppenstall's varied output is a single poem in an anthology of thirties verse, and his monograph on Raymond Roussel. None of Heppenstall's novels, which slipped in and out of print during his lifetime, have been reissued since 1986, five years after his death. His debut novel, *The Blaze of Noon*, was translated into several European languages during the author's lifetime; its first edition carried an introduction by Elizabeth Bowen, immediately selling out and proving a considerable critical success. It was later cited by no less a critic than Hélène Cixous as the novel which founded the *nouveau roman*.

I discovered Rayner Heppenstall in spring 2003, almost by accident. Despite my passion for the works of his close friend George Orwell, and my familiarity with many of Heppenstall's literary acquaintances (not least Dylan Thomas), I had never heard of Heppenstall until I chanced on John Carey's vitriolic diatribe in *The Intellectuals and the Masses*. The book's transparently conservative aesthetic agenda had, for me, the opposite of its intended effect of discouraging readers from tackling supposedly 'difficult' authors. I was greatly intrigued by Carey's brief discussion of Heppenstall in his postscript, suspecting (correctly) that his broadside against the author was deliberately misleading, motivated primarily by

Carey's formally conservative literary prejudices.

The first Heppenstall novel I read was *The Lesser Infortune*, a novel about the Second World War that never left the British Isles, which seemed to have plenty in common with the French works I was reading (in translation), its narrative rarely breaking from the confines of the protagonist's psychology. This was the only one held at the University of Manchester, where I was an undergraduate – unknown to me at the time, the University of Leeds just across the Pennines held all of his published works, as well as an archive of his journals and correspondence. Unmentioned by Carey (either because he found it contained none of the problematic ideology with which he was determined to smear Heppenstall, or perhaps because he simply had not read it), I soon found that this was perhaps the most obscure of Heppenstall's novels, largely evading contemporary reviewers and never reissued after its publication in 1953.

Finding this 'forgotten' novel a joy to read, I sought out more of Heppenstall's fiction. After enjoying his translation of Roussel's *Impressions of Africa*, *The Blaze of Noon* was the next novel I tracked down. This deceptively simple story about a blind masseur conjured up an atmosphere unlike that of any other novel I had ever read, an invigorating blend of arrogance and insecurity, epressed in a beautifully distilled, idiosyncratic prose style that hinted at a wide range of influences and yet felt entirely unique; it confirmed to me that Heppenstall was an author with whom I would become intimately acquainted.

The University of Sussex, where I started my Masters that autumn, had a far better selection of Heppenstall's novels (including *The Lesser Infortune*, which, it seemed, had never been borrowed), as well as his journals. These familiarised me with the name of B. S. Johnson, who came to play an incredibly important role in my project. Another 'forgotten' novelist writing 'experimental' works in post-war Britain, Johnson was undergoing a high-profile rediscovery just as I was ploughing my own furrow on one of his contemporaries.

I read Johnson's writings alongside Heppenstall's, and discovered a whole circle of obscure avant-garde novelists and poets through Johnson's tireless, inspirational championing of their individual and collective causes. I learned through Heppenstall's journals that Johnson considered him a 'father figure' to this 'experimental' circle, giving Heppenstall drafts of his early novels to read and striking up an important, if often fractious, exchange of ideas with the foremost British expert on the *nouveau roman*. Having read Orwell and Dylan Thomas, as well as the French authors that Heppenstall so admired, I had found another context within which Heppenstall could be read – one that I was invited to speak on at a conference on B. S. Johnson and his circle organised by Philip Tew, whose critical study was the first published work on Johnson.

It was there that I met Jonathan Coe, whose long-awaited biography had done much to instigate this surge of interest in Johnson and drawn numerous glowing reviews, not least from myself. Telling him that I was writing my Masters dissertation on Rayner Heppenstall, we discussed our projects, his published, mine unrealised, much as (I like to think) Johnson and Heppenstall would have discussed theirs. Talking about which authors within Johnson's circle were 'remembered', and which we liked, Coe confided that he had never read Heppenstall's fiction, but had consulted Rayner's journals as research, finding highly dubious speculations (not least that Johnson and Ann Quin, who died weeks before Johnson, were having an affair) and temporal inaccuracies, maintaining that there was no way that Heppenstall could have seen Johnson's film *Fat Man on a Beach* at the point he discusses it. These journals, I explained, were written during a difficult period in Heppenstall's later life, beset by depression, financial anxieties and professional disillusionment, and should not deter him from Heppenstall's earlier fiction, which was considered delicate and often strikingly inventive.

I sent Coe my review, and my paper. He replied that, regarding his book, 'One of my main regrets now is that I didn't put more about Heppenstall in it. Your article made him sound quite fascinating...the best kind of subject for a biography, really.' (This would be an interesting undertaking. Heppenstall publicised so much about his life in his memoirs that (like Coe's) any biography must necessarily investigate its own form, much as Heppenstall's novels ceaselessly explored theirs.) This gave me strength to find a supervisor for my work – a difficult task, as nobody at the university was familiar with Heppenstall's output.

Once I had done this, and sought out all of Heppenstall's novels (some of which, notably *The Connecting Door* and *Two Moons*, were particularly difficult to obtain), I tracked down all the critical assessments of Heppenstall's novels that I could find. This amounted to a brief article by Julian Symons in the *London Review of Books*, a couple of paragraphs in a 1967 article by Cixous, and articles by Jeremy Green and Adalgisa Giorgio that ultimately proved elusive. If studies of British literature from the thirties to the present day mentioned Heppenstall at all, (and very few of them did), it was usually the briefest of asides, most often referring to *The Blaze of Noon* or *The Connecting Door* – I found no reference anywhere to his war novels, or The Woodshed, and only Carey's damning indictments of his final novels, *Two Moons* and *The Pier*.

I spent the summer of 2005 writing in my study, delving deep into Heppenstall's often eccentric opinions and complex literary relationships, becoming thoroughly familiar with the nuances of his distinctive prose style (particularly his refusal to use semi-colons or dashes), and with the diverse range of influences, relentless investigations into the consciousness of the self, and the instinctive distrust of any ideology or belief system that characterised his novels.

This is, of course, the first published study of Rayner Heppenstall. Its aim is to reintroduce his novels both to literary critics and the wider public, on both sides of the Atlantic. Hopefully, it will also engender further interest in his fascinating critical work and his contribution to the development of British radio. There is much work to do. The BBC rejected my proposal for a radio documentary on Heppenstall and his work on the *Third Programme* (showing a disappointing lack of regard for its own heritage, perhaps because they felt Heppenstall represented the Reithian ideal of broadcasting as a means of 'cultural uplift', highly unfashionable in contemporary Britain) and despite the surge of interest in B. S. Johnson and the continued fascination with both Orwell and Dylan Thomas, not even Heppenstall's candid memoirs detailing these relationships are currently in print.

I met Hélène Cixous at a conference at the University of Sussex in 2006, and questioned her about Heppenstall. She told me that she had not read Heppenstall, or any of the other writers of 'le roman expérimental en Grand Bretagne' since the mid-sixties, adding that she did not even know what had happened to the author of *The Blaze of Noon*. This, to me, seemed sadly representative of Heppenstall's complete loss to literary history – even his most ardent, and most celebrated champion had not followed (or been able to follow) the course of his life or career.

Now seems as appropriate a time as any to remind ourselves of Heppenstall's existence. His novels were often under-appreciated in their own time, with *The Blaze of Noon* and *Saturnine* in particular failing to make the critical impact they deserved, being obscured by the outbreak of war. Heppenstall's pessimism about the place of experimental or innovative writing within the English cultural landscape seems even more prescient in the early twentieth century than it did when he was writing, given the anxiety about the 'dumbing-down' of British culture that seems to concern everyone except those that operate within the nation's key cultural institutions. This situation is one that I deeply hope will be reversed.

I also hope that the critical void around Rayner Heppenstall will be filled, just as the void around Raymond Roussel has been since Heppenstall wrote his pioneering study. Many of Heppenstall's contemporaries in Britain's post-war 'experimental' circles are also under-studied, under-valued and under-published. The time has come to re-evaluate an entire culture

of inventive, progressive literature that has all too often, and all too successfully been ignored or maligned by critics with a reactionary agenda.
B. S. Johnson has the critical re-appraisal that his fascinating, invigorating
novels deserve – and so too, finally, does Rayner Heppenstall.

Acknowledgements

I must thank Nicholas Royle of the University of Sussex, who kindly volunteered to supervise my Masters dissertation despite his unfamiliarity with Heppenstall's work; he soon became enthralled with *The Blaze of Noon*, offering much encouragement and no little insight regarding my work. Susanna Sklepek kindly translated Cixous' crucial article, and Jeremy M. Davies of the Dalkey Archive Press proved immeasurably helpful in seeing this project to fruition. D. J. Taylor, the Orwell biographer, helpfully corresponded with me about Heppenstall's life and works; Sam Thomas provided much-needed moral support, as did my dear friend Joe Stretch.

I must also show my appreciation of those who made this publication possible. Firstly, I must thank the Leeds Philosophical and Literary Society for their kind financial assistance, along with Donald and Lindy Foord, both for their generous patronage and for granting permission to quote extensively from Heppenstall's works. Finally, I must thank my parents, and my grandmother, who was a keen listener to BBC Radio during its 'Golden Age' to which Heppenstall contributed so much.

Rayner Heppenstall:
A Critical Guide

> 'In this country, there is too little technical enterprise.
> We have endless conventional novels.'[1]

So wrote Rayner Heppenstall in 1961, exasperated by England's failure to produce a literary movement comparable to the French *nouveau roman*. Born in Huddersfield on 27 July 1911, Heppenstall studied English and Modern Languages at the University of Leeds, cultivating a lifelong passion for French literature. During his professional life he was a journalist, broadcaster, critic, and a novelist, writing eight in total. After issuing several volumes of poetry, Heppenstall published his first novel, *The Blaze of Noon*, in 1939. His subsequent fictional output was sporadic: *Saturnine* appeared in 1943, while Heppenstall was in the Army; its sequel, *The Lesser Infortune*, was not published for another decade. Rayner did not release another novel until 1962, when both *The Connecting Door* and *The Woodshed* were issued, before *The Shearers* in 1969. Eight years later, *Two Moons* appeared, and his final novel, *The Pier*, was published posthumously. Rayner Heppenstall died in Deal on 23 May 1981.

Heppenstall's denunciation of England's 'endless conventional novels' eloquently captured the frustration many upcoming writers felt, with the formally reactionary 'Angry Young Men' becoming the darlings of post-war literary critics. Often aggressively philistine, these authors disdained Modernism, claiming that the experimentation of Joyce, Woolf and others had pushed the novel into a cul-de-sac that could only be escaped by returning to the forms popular during the Victorian period.

---

1   Rayner Heppenstall, *The Fourfold Tradition* (Barrie & Rockliff: London 1961), p270.

As he expressed his dissatisfaction, Heppenstall was writing a novel that deliberately accentuated the influence of Alain Robbe-Grillet, the *nouveau roman* figurehead, upon its construction in an attempt to produce a British equivalent. His articulation of sympathy with the *nouveau roman* in *The Fourfold Tradition*, and its creative manifestation in *The Connecting Door*, prompted critics to define Heppenstall as an 'experimental' novelist, and he won the attention of several younger writers aiming to rehabilitate modernist writing. These included Anthony Burgess, Alan Burns, Eva Figes, Ann Quin and B. S. Johnson, who included Rayner in his conscious attempt to create a circle of writers unified by their hatred of formal conservatism. Johnson loathed the term 'experimental', believing that 'to most reviewers [it] is almost always a synonym for "unsuccessful"'[2]: these counter-traditionalists would best be described as 'neo-Modernists', given their shared interest in continuing the inter-war investigation into the possibilities of literary form.

Johnson was their ringleader, championing Sterne, Joyce and especially Samuel Beckett, whose output could justifiably be situated within both Anglo-Irish and French Modernist contexts. Like Beckett, Heppenstall was fluent in both English and French, and although he never published in French, his novels usually demonstrated the influence of French-language writing, often referencing French authors. In his critical volumes (particularly *The Fourfold Tradition*) he highlighted intrinsic similarities and parallel trends with-in English and French writing, within both traditional and counter-traditional literatures.

The Connecting Door, labelled an 'anti-novel' by its publisher, (as the *nouveau roman* also became known outside France), did not just attract the attention of Johnson's circle, which shared Heppenstall's admiration

---

2   B. S. Johnson, *Aren't You Rather Young to be Writing Your Memoirs?* (Hutchinson: London 1973), p19.

for this French neo-Modernism.[3] Even before its release suggested affinities with Robbe-Grillet, one or two critics had suggested that *The Blaze of Noon*, Heppenstall's debut novel, inaugurated the *nouveau roman*. These critics were often European. British commentators, even those reconsidering the novel during the sixties, tended to stress the influence of D. H. Lawrence and Henry Miller, retrospectively placing it within a tradition of Anglo-American Modernist writing rather than asking how it anticipated developments in post-war continental literature.

Until the sixties, Heppenstall had avoided clarifying his literary preferences, having befriended many important cultural figures, including Eric Gill, John Middleton Murry, Dylan Thomas and most famously, George Orwell. It is for his account of a drunken *contretemps* with Orwell, published in *Four Absentees*, where Heppenstall describes Orwell's look of 'fear and sadistic exaltation' as his flatmate raises a shooting-stick above his head, that Rayner is most often discussed, frequently troubling Orwell biographers.[4] Orwell and Heppenstall remained friends, but many British critics formed an unfavorable opinion of Heppenstall's character, based on revelations in his memoirs and (especially) his posthumously published journals, as well as the ideological tone of his final novels, *Two Moons* and *The Pier*. Consequently, Heppenstall has all but vanished from British literary history, his novels absent from university reading lists and entirely out of print. The Anglo-American liberal-pluralist revision of the canon, opposing the domination of university syllabi by 'dead white men', has often focused on ensuring greater minority representation rather than encouraging the reassessment of an author or text's place within narrative(s) of formal innovation.

When British critics have discussed Heppenstall, they have often appropiated him to illustrate Modernism's more sinister tendencies, and

---

3   Heppenstall, *The Intellectual Part* (Barrie & Rockliff: London 1963), p209.

4   Heppenstall, *Four Absentees* (Sphere: London 1988), p59.

even then, only in passing. Populist critic John Carey devoted two pages to castigating Heppenstall in the postscript to *The Intellectuals and the Masses*, a simplistic, contentious study of the complex relationship between Modernism, elitism, and right-wing extremism, which characterised Nietzsche as the Machiavellian demon behind all three. Focusing primarily on Heppenstall's final novels and journals, Carey explains how he relished 'contemplating the extinction of large sections of humanity', which apparently informed Heppenstall's malicious decision to make his writing 'defiantly difficult'.[5] Additionally, Carey deliberately misrepresents *The Blaze of Noon*'s ironic references to Nietzsche and, ignoring his other novels, dishonestly implies that Rayner (who fought in World War Two) was a lifelong Fascist.

For Hélène Cixous, however, Heppenstall was a captivating figure, worthy of considerable praise. Engaged solely with form, Cixous did not just share Heppenstall's belief that 'experimental' writing in England and France were closely linked; she became the most prominent critic to name the Englishman as the founder of the *nouveau roman*. In an article for *Le Monde* on '*le roman experiméntal*' in Britain, published in May 1967, Cixous likened Heppenstall's novels to those of Michel Butor, stating that '*il à inauguré le nouveau roman dès 1939 avec* The Blaze of Noon'.[6] Cixous also praised '*Porte de communication*', simultaneously crediting Heppenstall with a pivotal role in the development of the French *nouveau roman* and within the subsequent British neo-Modernist project, to which Heppenstall, although peripherally involved, never wholeheartedly committed.

Heppenstall found several of these British authors – particularly Burns and Johnson – disagreeably tendentious, disliking their tendency to link aesthetic radicalism with revolutionary politics. Perhaps this was why the

---

5   John Carey, *The Intellectuals and the Masses: Pride and Prejudice among the Literary Intelligentsia 1880-1939* (Faber & Faber: London 1992), p210.

6   Hélène Cixous, 'Langage et regard dans le roman experimental: Grand-Bretagne' in *Le Monde,* 6959.viia. (18 May 1967), p16.

nouveau roman was the only contemporary literary development that he unconditionally championed after flirting with, and ultimately rejecting, numerous ideologies, philosophies, and movements. Like Heppenstall, these writers prioritised formal innovation above political commitment, rejecting Sartre's concept of 'engagement' and demanding that the *nouveau roman* be 'a free and autonomous process of discovery'.[7]

The *nouveau roman* had no manifesto, and was not unified by a pre-determined set of principles like futurism or surrealism. The movement was a critical invention (which perhaps explains its vague name), with reviewers discerning similarities in Robbe-Grillet, Butor, Nathalie Sarraute, Claude Simon, Marguerite Duras, and others, all opposed to the 'traditional' novel, resenting Socialist realism, and all publishing at least one novel through Editions de Minuit. 'Anti-novels' such as Robbe-Grillet's *The Erasers* (1953), *In the Labyrinth* (1957) and *Jealousy* (1957), as well as Sarraute's *The Planetarium* (1959) and *The Golden Fruits* (1963), and Simon's *The Flanders Road* (1957) seemed to lack the components of 'conventional' novels – dramatic plots, coherent temporality and complex exploration of character psychology – that had been carried into much Modernist literature, focusing instead on concrete objects and the mundane, random events of everyday life. Often exploring the limitations of writing, its narrative material took place 'in the reflective consciousness of the novelist', examining the relationship between the internal working of the author's psyche and problematic concepts of 'reality'.[8]

The Blaze of Noon and *The Connecting Door* received the most attention on their original release and when the *nouveau roman* was at its most fashionable. Of all his novels, they have been the most studied. His other 'earlier' novels – *Saturnine*, *The Lesser Infortune* and *The Woodshed* – have all

---

7   Celia Britton, *The Nouveau roman: Fiction, theory and politics* (MacMillan: London/ Basingstoke 1992), p31.

8   John Sturrock, *The French New Novel: Claude Simon, Michel Butor, Alain Robbe-Grillet* (OUP: Oxford 1969), p19.

fallen obscure despite possessing many admirable qualities, although now, with British neo-Modernism having frequently been unfavorably judged, Heppenstall's novels have undeservedly become equally and almost totally forgotten. For those interested in the *nouveau roman*, domestic (neo-)Modernism and the project of reconsidering the canon of formally inventive British literature, and the criteria by which authors are included within it, Rayner Heppenstall demands reassessment: a reassessment that must begin with his debut.

Hesitations of the Eye:

The Blaze of Noon *and the Writing of the Thirties*

'I also had a theoretical notion that the cinema had taken over the story-telling functions of the exteriorised novel and that prose narrative would do well to become more lyrical, more inward.'[9]

Heppenstall's debut novel appeared at a time when British intellectuals were in a state of despair. The optimism regarding the influence of literary creativity upon active politics that characterised the thirties, encapsulated in intense intellectual politicization and opposition to governmental policies on the rise of fascism, the Spanish Civil War, appeasement and unemployment, had dissipated amidst the victory of Franco, the Nazi-Soviet Pact and the outbreak of war.

It was in this context that Heppenstall established himself as a writer. For much of the decade, he was perceived as a poet, despite his short monograph on Middleton Murry and the ballet study *Apology for Dancing*. His *First Poems* (1935) demonstrated affinities with Yeats, French Symbolism and (particularly) T. S. Eliot more than Auden and Spender (usually cast as the poetic orthodoxy of the period) or his close friend Dylan Thomas. Often explicitly religious (many were written during Heppenstall's brief dalliance with Catholicism), his verse only occasionally engaged with politics, and when it did, as in 'Risorgimento', it avoided specific social critique. Rather, it established an atmosphere in which any form of belief is undermined by an event which renders faith impossible, or a malignant, intangible being that threatens the isolated, agnostic individual. Whilst there are optimistic moments, particularly when political and religious imagery coalesce, 'Mary of Magdala' is not atypical:

---

9   Heppenstall, *The Blaze of Noon* (Sphere: London 1967), p6.

> There is no voice to comfort me:
> No voice in my ears
> But a cry that strains the substance of a cross.[10]

The deeply metaphysical *Sebastian* (1937) was an epic, in which Heppenstall expounded his established themes. While this form did not always recapture the concentrated energy of his short verses, the not unsuccessful realisation of this ambitious project confirmed Heppenstall's critical reputation as a promising young writer.

His criticism for *Adelphi*, the *New English Weekly* and Eliot's *Criterion* helped Rayner form defining relationships with prominent literary personalities and various contemporary trends and movements. Heppenstall was aware of the British surrealist movement in poetry and painting headed by the artist Roland Penrose and the young poet David Gascoyne. His friends Dylan Thomas and Herbert Read, although not committed to the (short-lived) British surrealist project, were present at the International Surrealist Exhibition held at the New Burlington Galleries, London, in 1936. Lectures were delivered by Read, André Breton, Salvador Dalí, Paul Éluard, and fellow Yorkshireman Hugh Sykes Davies, who wrote the first British surrealist novel, *Petron*, in 1935. Reviewing *Petron*, which he declared was 'not a work of 'importance'', Heppenstall labelled surrealism 'a comprehensive technique of irresponsibility'. Writing as Hitler entrenched his power shortly before the Spanish War and the Stalinist Trials, Heppenstall demonstrated some belief in the social power of intellectual productivity, but even amongst this political turbulence he refused to deny such 'elaborate irresponsibility' a place within modern literature. Although Heppenstall's subsequent novels could never be described as 'surrealist', they display far more sympathy towards the surrealists' anti-rationality

---

10   'Mary of Magdala' in Heppenstall, *Poems 1933-1945* (Secker & Warburg: London 1946), p92.

and interest in the fantastical possibilities of the human psyche than with the social realist literature of novelists such as Walter Greenwood that ran counter to it during the thirties.[11]

Michael Sayers, an Irish writer who had seen his earlier aborted efforts, assured Heppenstall that he could never write a novel. Sayers, besides this challenge, also provided a subject, having told his ex-flatmate about a blind masseur in attendance on his mother. Heppenstall completed his novel amidst the Munich crisis; it was published on 10 November 1939, during the 'Phoney War'. Its publishers, Secker & Warburg, entitled it *The Blaze of Noon*, after its epigraph from *Paradise Lost*, and procured a foreword from Elizabeth Bowen, then personally unacquainted with Heppenstall. Given Bowen's critical reputation, this was quite a coup, but under the circumstances, her recommendation alone may not have been enough to earn the novel widespread recognition. The response of *The Evening Standard*, however, guaranteed publicity:

> 'frankest' novel is challenge to the censor
> AN AFFRONT TO DECENCY

The newspaper claimed that it was the most sexually explicit novel since *Lady Chatterley's Lover*; it immediately sold out.[12] Other reviewers did not comprehend *The Standard*'s moral outrage, believing *The Blaze of Noon* serious and intelligent. It remains intriguing: its unorthodox subject and its combination of English-language influences such as Miller and Lawrence with French writers like Louis-Ferdinand Céline, Marcel Jouhandeau, and (especially) Henry de Montherlant distinguish it from most other late Modernist or thirties novels.

'In form, *The Blaze of Noon* is an orthodox novel...but really it is a book

---

11   Heppenstall, 'Petron' in *The Criterion* Vol. XV (1935), pp333-334.

12   *Intellectual Part,* p43.

about sex', wrote Julian Symons in 1981.[13] Symons was perhaps influenced by Heppenstall's own declaration, introducing the 1962 edition, that it was 'a very simple book' and 'not the work of a literary theorist'.[14] Symons took him at face value, but not all reviewers considered it as 'simple' as its author suggested in a moment of characteristic self-deprecation. In 1963, Heppenstall noted an Italian critic who named him '*il padre del nouveau roman*', believing this trend was 'derived from a novel recounted in the first person by a blind man'.[15] Heppenstall, typically, refused this assertion, perhaps feeling that his novel would subsequently be judged only in relation to the works of the '*école du regard*' if accepted, rather than purely on its own merits.

It is this 'first person' narration and the impairment of the narrator, that accounts for such claims, and allows it to become far more than merely 'a book about sex'. Symons disliked the protagonist's 'creepy sexual magic' (as he saw it), and bemoaned the absence of 'direct description' of sexual intercourse, but this denied the subtlety by which Heppenstall posited sexuality within a complex relationship between intellectual reflection, emotional passion, and physical apprehension of the world.[16] Its opening sentences establish an erotically charged atmosphere, immediately privileging the sense of touch. 'The handshake and a few words of conversation are enough. I rarely fail to receive the impression of a woman on meeting her'.[17] The tone of this opening paragraph presents a façade of certainty, which narrator Louis Dunkel subtly undermines by stating 'I *rarely* fail', hinting towards a fundamental psychological insecurity that will eventu-

---

13   Julian Symons, 'Beyond Everyday Life' in *The London Review of Books*, Vol. III (March 1981), p20.

14   *Blaze of Noon*, p6.

15   *Intellectual Part*, p212.

16   Symons, p20.

17   *Blaze of Noon,* p9.

ally overwhelm him. Here, Dunkel explains how these signifiers help him determine a woman's age, character, and physical attributes with a commendable degree of accuracy. The reliability of his sensory perception is queried in the next paragraph, when he explains that he cannot determine this for men. Although Louis' disability is not mentioned until its second page, it becomes clear that the novel is primarily about *blindness*: the attendant uncertainty of knowledge is expressed in appropriately delicate, sceptical and often ironic prose, which was to become distinctive, even if it did not attempt to create its own radically new textual style in staunch opposition to 'traditional' literature in the manner of Joyce, Woolf or John Dos Passos.

The Blaze of Noon concentrated its opposition to formal convention upon structure rather than language. The structural *centre* of the narrative fixes the novel's form: Heppenstall's choice of central figure anchors its narrative content, the position taken on its events, and which issues arise from them. Heppenstall is acutely aware that 'All value is first constituted by a theoretical subject'.[18] Louis' blindness required heightened awareness of objects, manifested in lengthy descriptions that emphasised their properties above any metaphysical 'significance' that also characterised Robbe-Grillet's writing. The importance of such properties to Dunkel is initially established not by the presence but by the crucial *absence* of information. The lack of a handshake means that 'of the girl Sophie Madron, sitting behind me, I could create no definite image,' and she remains a point of fascination for him throughout.[19] Heppenstall immediately establishes that the material world can never be certain for Dunkel, the reader's point of identification. This uncertainty necessitates and fixes both the unorthodox formalization of its narration and the central problem that this narration

---

18   Jacques Derrida, 'Force and Signification' in *Writing and Difference* (Routledge: London 2003), p32.

19   *Blaze of Noon*, p10.

addresses: the search for self-definition amidst a modernity too complex for any individual to comprehend.

Dunkel's sexual relations, inevitably complicated by his blindness, play an important role in this search for self-definition. These complications are not always negative, however. Louis' sense of touch, necessarily refined, maximises the pleasure both parties derive from sex. Nowhere is this sensitivity more salient than when Louis describes the build up to intercourse. In the novel's strongest description of sexual interaction, Louis recalls how 'I put the palms of my hands to her breasts, touching them to the side and below, without moving her at all. Her breasts were clear and unmauled, fully ripe without any falling weight.'[20] This restrained prose possesses a genuine lyricism, betraying Heppenstall's origins as a poet. This lyricism could not have been sustained if he had succumbed to the 'temptation to talk instead about a good fuck', as Henry Miller often did and as Symons suggested Heppenstall should.[21] Rather, Dunkel halts his description at its climactic point to ask 'what are the emotions?' and offer a series of reflections on how 'civilised man' relates to his emotional impulses, refuting Lawrence's belief that 'we must become more animal.'[22]

It is these *gaps* in Louis' accounts, and Heppenstall's filling them with restless interrogation of numerous subjects as they relate to sexuality and human consciousness, that raise his novel above *The Standard*'s portrayal of it as pornography. *The Standard* grudgingly acknowledged that *The Blaze of Noon* was well written and contained much that was praiseworthy, something which caused their reviewer genuine consternation. 'The problem for the censor remains', the newspaper stated, 'has public toleration of

---

20   *Blaze of Noon*, p68.

21   Symons, p20.

22   *Blaze of Noon,* p70.

what used to be considered indecent literature advanced so far that a book like this [has become acceptable]?'[23] *The Standard*'s critic had not missed the aesthetic qualities of Heppenstall's novel amidst his moralistic fury, but was not prepared to lay down his prudish opposition to its sexual content in acknowledgement of its literary value.

Paul de Man noted that the 'moments of greatest blindness…are also the moments at which [critics] achieve their greatest insight.'[24] Louis' actual (rather than metaphorical) blindness has necessitated and accentuated an analytical mania, visible through a mode of narration that often intertwines extended intellectual reflection with descriptions of objects. The novel's 'form' and 'content' cannot easily be separated. The prose style employed by Heppenstall, and the focus on the introverted consciousness of Louis Dunkel, are dictated by the subject matter.

Deliberating upon his own sexual practices, Dunkel declares that 'to make love in a state of emotional tension is…a disease to which Englishmen of the middle classes and especially of the lower middle classes are notably prone.'[25] Here, Dunkel hints towards the socio-political issue that Heppenstall addresses: the position of the *bourgeoisie* at a time when the values that upheld bourgeois society have collapsed, threatening its attendant liberal-democratic infrastructure. *The Blaze of Noon* is a bourgeois novel, its focus being upon the mundane objects and realities of everyday middle-class existence. This differentiates it from much thirties literature, often concerned with proletarian life and informed by socialist ideology, and anticipates Robbe-Grillet's belief that 'the function of art is never to illustrate [an ideological] truth…but to bring into the world certain

---

23   *Intellectual Part*, p43.

24   Paul de Man, 'The Rhetoric of Blindness: Jacques Derrida's Reading of Rousseau' in *Blindness and Insight: Essays in the Rhetoric of Contemporary Criticism* (Routledge: London 1986), p109.

25   *Blaze of Noon,* p70.

interrogations.'[26] The issue of class and the class sympathies adopted by the period's competing ideologies does affect Louis, but does not dictate his sympathies as might be expected. He is demonstrably bourgeois; given his background, one may not be surprised to hear him advocate conservative policies, but he remains skeptical about any politicisation. Instead, Louis prefers to identify himself with Modernist art, itself threatened by both fascism and Stalinism; for Dunkel, who never discusses recent Communist cultural policy, fascism in particular. It is intriguing that Heppenstall chose such a Germanic-sounding surname for his protagonist – Dunkel's upbringing is spent in Norwich, and it is never suggested that his background is anything other than English. Louis displays awareness of Picasso, Dalí and Kandinsky (ironically, as he can only imagine how they subverted artistic convention), and a taste for modern, French-based composers Auric, Milhaud and Stravinsky.[27] It is this culture that he strives to protect from philistine ideology, Left or Right: he explains to fascist Trevor Beed that 'the French...might teach us about leading the civilised life.'[28] Crucially, Dunkel fears that fascism will put a stop to cultural interchange between Britain and Europe, and that conservative appeasement will not prevent this eventuality. However, his impairment and his inability to alter Beed's ideological position reinforce his sense of futility, and his intense pessimism about the ability of the cultured intellectual to intervene decisively in political concerns.

There are several political discussions in *The Blaze of Noon*, but Dunkel offers no prioritising of opinions. Mrs Nance offers her views on revolutionary politics, telling Louis: 'that's where the revolution is coming from in this country...not from the working classes but from dispossessed,

---

26   Alain Robbe-Grillet, 'The Use of Theory' in *For a New Novel: Essays on Fiction* (Grove Press: New York 1965), p14.

27   *Blaze of Noon,* p21.

28   Ibid, p58.

class-conscious rich boys. They'll never be content until they've got their own back on the working classes, smashed their organisations and bled them down to what they were a hundred years ago.'[29] Louis attempts to absolve himself, reflecting 'I am not myself implicated in these questions. The excessively rich are my employers, and I myself am classless, though I have affinities with the intolerably poor' – his disability has distanced him from his bourgeois origins, but he resists identifying with 'the proletariat', a very different ideological concept to 'the poor'.[30]

Heppenstall believed that Gide opened 'an explosion of individual consciousness brought about by the discovery that the world was not un-changing...so that it could no longer be merely observed.'[31] Gide, like most modernist writers, was bourgeois, examining the lives of middle-class individuals existing within the political and intellectual turbulence of *fin-de-siècle* and twentieth century Europe. The focus on internal con-sciousness in *The Blaze of Noon* situates it within a discourse of (British and French) bourgeois writing, running from the nineteenth century to the late thirties. Barthes believed that Camus and Blanchot represented 'the last episode of a passion of writing' that encompassed Balzac, Château-briand, Zola and Naturalism, Mallarmé and the Symbolists, Gide, Proust, and the surrealists, concluding with 'colourless' writing informed by an awareness that serving literary writing to ideological ends had facilitated its implication in totalitarian atrocities.[32] Heppenstall was versed in this French discourse (he later translated Balzac, Châteaubriand, and Rous-sel, whom he discovered after the war) but his novel also engaged with a parallel English history of 'realist' tradition and various counter-traditions, culminating in fragmented strands in thirties literature nominally headed

---

29   Ibid, p17.

30   Ibid, p18.

31   *Fourfold Tradition*, p114.

32   Roland Barthes, *Writing Degree Zero* (Jonathan Cape: London 1967), p11.

by Auden and Spender, Orwell, Robert Graves, David Gascoyne, Wynd-ham Lewis, and Eliot. *The Blaze of Noon*, however, did not sit comfortably with any of them.

The political changes since 1935, when he reviewed *Petron*, meant that Heppenstall did not feel compelled to produce a work of social 'impor-tance'. The novel's sense of resignation about the future of the artistic discourse that had produced Modernism and Socialist Realism is deftly illustrated by the irony of Louis reading Nietzsche, so inspirational for many English and French Modernists, in Braille.[33] He also reads Eliot thusly. His self-conscious use of this psychologically internalised prose style – one characterised by the Socialist Realists as inherently bourgeois – suggested that Heppenstall was aware that this literary discourse would expire amidst the forthcoming war, an awareness that informed *The Blaze of Noon*'s political restraint and cautious engagement with modern fiction.

Heppenstall's narrator, unlike those of realist novels, does not merely observe: he ceaselessly analyses and adopts peculiar positions on contem-porary ideas. In doing so, Louis is less disadvantaged as he understands Braille, and so can read (translated) works of modern philosophy like anyone else. Unusually, Dunkel engages with Freud and Nietzsche, form-ing idiosyncratic opinions on their crucial tenets. He virtually ignores Marx, the other dominant intellectual influence upon thirties literature. His relationship with these ideas is sophisticated: he displays an impressive working knowledge of Freud, intermittently recounting psychoanalytical ideas to help him interpret his own actions. Contemplating his own (nor-mally reliable) memory and its lapses, he reflects that 'Dr. Freud [taught] that if we forget some episode in our own lives…that was because our mind rejected it as something disturbing.'[34] His intellectual interests affect the way he interacts with people on a daily basis, rather than leading him

---

33   *Blaze of Noon*, p26.

34   Ibid, p125.

into any 'movement', something which is perceived by his acquaintances. Exasperated by Louis' treatment of Amity and Sophie, Mrs. Nance asks, 'You're not coming all over Nietzschean, are you?...You're not cultivating the rights of the superior man...taking just what you want wherever you can find it?'[35] Louis feels ashamed, but he offers no apology or self-justification, and remains indifferent towards Mrs. Nance's attempt to cast him as an aspirant *übermensch*.

The Blaze of Noon's most radical gesture was to question bourgeois sexual morality, perhaps an unsurprising point of investigation given its engagement with Freud and Nietzsche. Mrs. Nance's assessment of nephew John's relationship with fiancée Betty des Voeux sets Louis thinking about conservative conceptions of gender roles and power. Mrs. Nance tells Louis: '[Betty] keeps up this new, mixed game of bohemian morals and landed-gentry manners...she sleeps with John when she feels like it', unfavourably contrasting her values with those of 'the pure, wilting girls of the generation before mine.'[36] Here, Louis presents himself as having no opinion on Betty's forcefulness – the fact that he has only just arrived provides an excuse not to state a position. However, he privately contemplates sexual morality at length: he unceasingly questions social constructions of masculinity and femininity, without condemning men considered effeminate, and tacitly condoning women who use their sexuality to combat subjugation rooted in and justified by traditional morality. A patient confides: 'If I showed any signs of enjoying [sex], my husband would consider me...a whore'. Louis is disappointed that she does not add 'And a whore is precisely what I should be.'[37] This is not a misogynistic disapproval of a woman who conceives sex primarily as an enjoyable act. Rather, Dunkel suggests (at least to himself) that she should turn this op-

---

35   Ibid, p140.

36   Ibid, p17.

37   Ibid, p96.

pressive idea against itself, by making her sexual pleasure abundantly clear to her husband, who would then be forced to reconsider his position. Thus, Heppenstall takes the woman's internalisation of this patriarchal expedient and intelligently inverts it, suggesting how it could be used as a weapon. Homosexual characters make fleeting appearances, and whilst a marriage in which a lesbian wife and homosexual man is criticised as 'a convenient framework within which each...could seduce the other's unsuspecting friends',[38] the possibility that Mrs. Tralee's daughter may harbour lesbian desires for Sophie is considered without prejudice.[39] This is typical of the novel's equivocal, even-handed criticism of the morality that curtails sexual freedom. Even given the greater acceptance of sexual diversity among thirties literary circles, *The Blaze of Noon*'s attitude to sexuality was commendably progressive.

This idiosyncratic engagement with ideas is not limited to Dunkel's position on philosophical or intellectual theories. Heppenstall displays similar ambivalence about the first-person narrator that he uses to structurally centre his novel. This becomes apparent when Louis openly questions his own position, admitting that the story that his arrival initiated has escaped his control. 'It would be the entry marked 14 June, and if this story had remained under my control that would have been the most important date in it' – as soon as Dunkel exhibits this ironic self-consciousness about his centrality, he ceases to narrate as before and switches to a diary format.[40] 'I found that I had got left behind by my own action and that the other actors in my story were so far ahead of me that it had already ceased to be my story in any but a purely technical sense', Louis regrets, realising that as narrator, he was supposed to fix the boundaries of the story, but

---

38   Ibid, p56.

39   Ibid, p29.

40   Ibid, p138.

his actions have strained those confines until they have collapsed.[41] He understands that his attempts at objectively analyzing his surroundings have failed, as he can never escape his own subjectivity, and characteristically, Louis becomes aware that a single individual can never control a narrative. He voluntarily reneges the privilege that he has bestowed upon his version of events, belatedly acknowledging that the other characters would have told his story differently. He concludes: 'The only thing is that if I allowed it to do so either I should have to cover dozens of pages with my own private reflections or...make a violent effort of the imagination to present all that happened from somebody else's point of view.'[42] This restrained investigation into the limitations of narrative construction anticipates strands in both British and French neo-Modernism (and post-Modernism), in Johnson's circle and the *nouveau roman*: rarely discussed, this metafictional self-consciousness about the problems of recording a narrative often informed the structural experimentation of Butor, Robbe-Grillet, and Sarraute, particularly in Sarraute's *The Golden Fruits*.

Louis is similarly perceptive of the reason why he must objectify the other characters: he is forced to interpret them using non-visual signifiers – both people and items inevitably assume the same status as objects in his attempt to define himself. Indeed, it is this awareness that leads him to question the validity of his narrative construction. Before Amity arrives, Louis resents the impending arrival of Mrs. Nance's blind, deaf, and dumb niece, particularly as the other residents at Rose Gwavas expect them to bond through their shared disability. Louis is repulsed: 'The thought of her was accompanied by thoughts of all the cumbrous and humiliating apparatus for the blind which I had exerted myself very strenuously to avoid...whose only purpose...is to turn the human being into a subject for

41   Ibid, p134.

42   Ibid.

demonstrations of popular science.'[43] His main preliminary concern is that Amity's presence will somehow strip him of his humanity. This is typical of the way Dunkel's introverted consciousness turns other characters into *ideas*, restraining their signification possibilities within the narrative structure that he creates and unsuccessfully attempts to control.

Dunkel conceives Amity as a perpetual child, forever mothered by caretaker Mrs. Brophy, whose philanthropy he believes to be malignant. However, his initial resistance to Amity subsides as he is forced to reconsider her relationship with Mrs. Brophy, and with the objects and traits that, for Louis, characterise her – her scent, her apparent Catholicism, her limited range of expression. Once Louis comprehends that Mrs. Brophy foists these upon Amity, making Amity an outlet for her dominant personality, he favorably reassesses Amity and, he believes, is seduced by her sensitivity. Here, Heppenstall's terse microcosm of human relations collapses: Dunkel alienates himself from his hosts by courting Amity before realising (long after everyone else) that he has used her to validate his ego. Louis admits that, 'My own mistake was to look for a decisive experience in Amity Nance, when all I had done was fall for a moment in love with the image of my own blindness.'[44] After arriving, she plays the pivotal role in challenging and developing Louis' attitudes to himself, and particularly to his sites of self-definition – his blindness and his touch – and so Louis falls in love with his own *idea* of Amity, not the 'reality' of Amity.

Louis, then, attempts to control the signification possibilities of other characters by fixing their meanings within terms that he establishes. However, what *Louis* represents, beyond the cultured European bourgeois, is not similarly fixed, as Heppenstall never attempts to suggest any 'meaning' for his protagonist who lies outside the boundaries of his own policing of signification. Dunkel's perceptions of himself, paradoxically, seem

---

43   Ibid, p34.

44   Ibid, p150.

even more unreliable than his perceptions of the material world, often contradicted by actions taken in states of heightened passion, such as his liaison with Amity, which cloud his apparently impeccable judgement. His unreliable world-perception is swiftly confessed; the fallibility of his self-perception is admitted later, once Louis is obliged to accept that his actions have had undesirable consequences for his hosts and for himself. His statement, 'Love is touch, and I am touch', an attempt to present himself as a master of sensitivity, is gradually undermined by his introspective lack of emotional awareness.[45]

Robbe-Grillet, aware of the manner in which ideologically subservient literature relied upon its characters carrying definite, fixed connotations, demanded that 'Instead of this universe of signification...we must try...to construct a world both more solid and more immediate.'[46] Louis' awareness that 'From the sense of touch...there is no escape...There is no innocent touch' fixed the novel's focus on the solid, immediate world, but did not entirely deny potential signification to its protagonist.[47] This statement, for example, suggests Dunkel's realisation that he is unable to avoid being assailed by guilt resulting from his interaction with wider society, despite his disability, which distanced him from it. Consequently, Louis could potentially represent anyone living in modernity, regardless of the comparative rarity of his affliction. Lawrence, the dominant British influence upon Heppenstall's novel, also centralised the figure of the 'blind man' in one of his short stories. Lawrence's eponymous *Blind Man* was a brooding, threatening presence whose eventual demonstration of humanity frightens his guest, in a narrative told in the third person. Blanchot, in *The Madness of the Day* (whose title curiously resembles *The Blaze of Noon*), also utilised the affliction of blindness for symbolic ends. This metaphor may seem

---

45   Ibid, p50.

46   Robbe-Grillet, 'A Future for the Novel', p21.

47   *Blaze of Noon*, p138.

rather unsubtle – the blind man exists in darkness – but its universality frees Louis and his narrative from appropriation into any ideological reading. He is, spiritually and intellectually, no more blind than anyone else, and so his resigned inability to sustain belief in *anything* represents the position of the European (particularly British) intellectuals in the late thirties.

The *nouveau roman* demanded interpretation 'in terms of the contemporary *Zeitgeist*', but not as an inevitable product of its age.[48] Robbe-Grillet declared that 'The writer must proudly consent to bear his own date, knowing that there are no masterpieces in eternity, but only works in history.'[49] *The Blaze of Noon*, despite being atypical of what has been retrospectively characterised as 'thirties' literature, was an intriguing product of its time, representing one particular conclusion to fervent Modernist experimentation, thirties ideological commitment, and any belief in the power of radicalised bourgeois intellectuals to revolutionise the world through art. It also deliberately distanced itself from an important trend within British Modernism: its attempted transposition of cinematic devices into literary prose. Modernist literature borrowed aesthetics from film, whilst inter-war mainstream film in Britain became highly literary, offering numerous adaptations of Victorian novels and plays, perhaps explaining Heppenstall's beliefs about its making the exteriorised narrative form redundant, an opinion that was shared by several *nouveau roman* authors, many of whom (unlike Heppenstall) also scripted or directed films that radically challenged the conventions of narrative cinema. Emphasising its own 'literary-ness', *The Blaze of Noon* deliberately investigated areas that were beyond the reach of the camera, hoping to discover new avenues for the bourgeois novel, and to an extent, it was successful – while displaying

48   Sturrock, p11.

49   Robbe-Grillet, 'The Use of Theory', p10.

an acute awareness of its specific intellectual and political context, *The Blaze of Noon* reads like no other work of its time.

It was Heppenstall's highly considered construction of his narrator, and his consequent textual prioritising of the physical qualities of objects and people rather than their signification, that allowed critics to perceive an antecedent of the *nouveau roman* in *The Blaze of Noon*. Inevitably, many aspects of the novel did not conform precisely to the model laid down in post-war France, but Robbe-Grillet believed 'considerable differences' in the works of those boxed within the *nouveau roman* movement to be 'a good thing', recognising that such differences within a 'movement' would help sustain its creative energy.[50] *The Blaze of Noon* was translated into French in 1947 — just before Sarraute published *Portrait of a Man Unknown*, for which Sartre popularized the term 'anti-novel' — as *L'Embrasement de Midi*, but Heppenstall stated his conviction that none of the prominent *nouveau roman* authors read it.[51] This could have been an attempt to mislead his critics, although he probably was not self-mythologising on this issue, and the crucial theoretical essays produced by those authors left Heppenstall unmentioned. Nevertheless, the novel found its way to influential critics such as Bowen and Cixous, who ensured it a position, however minor, within the history of the *nouveau roman*, and thus English *and* French 'experimental' writing.

This may not have happened without *The Evening Standard*'s indignant response, which publicised *The Blaze of Noon* at a time when it could have disappeared, but their portrayal of it as a 'story of poultry-yard morals' was misleading, diverting contemporary critics from its literary values.[52] 'The more ambivalent the original utterance, the more uniform and universal the consistent error in the followers and commentators', wrote de Man,

---

50   Robbe-Grillet, 'New Novel, New Man', p134.

51   *Intellectual Part*, p212.

52   Ibid, p43.

and the fascinatingly equivocal tone of Heppenstall's novel meant that it was repeatedly misinterpreted and underestimated, not least because Heppenstall repeatedly undersold it.[53] The novel won an Arts Council award in 1967 for works denied sufficient attention on publication; however, it moved in and out of print throughout Rayner's life, and has been deleted since his death. It has been largely excluded from literary histories of its decade – even the sympathetic Julian Symons fails to mention Heppenstall in his account of the period's intellectual culture, perhaps because he rejected the currents within thirties literature that Symons wanted to emphasise.

The (perhaps unfashionable) Christian belief that dominated Heppenstall's poetry constitutes a curious absence in *The Blaze of Noon*: indeed, the novel demonstrates a collapse of faith in the revolutionary power of any belief system, representing the end (or, at least, *an* end) to the thirties. The futility inherent in *The Blaze of Noon* hinted towards the difficulties in intellectual self-definition that characterised forties literature, a context in which it can also be read. In 1939, the future of the *world* was uncertain, as was the nature of the impending war: British authors knew only that it would be cataclysmic, and that now, an author's political involvement could just as easily (depending on age) involve active service as literary 'engagement'. The optimism that had previously infused some thirties literature had become unsustainable, its dissipation symbolised by the early deaths of several important cultural figures and the appearance of *Finnegan's Wake*, which (in Heppenstall's opinion) took the Modernist revolt to its negative conclusion, making a concerted attempt to destroy language itself. Amidst such uncertainty, nobody could begin to imagine what course modern literature would take. How could one concentrate on writing when the state of the world, and one's own life, was at stake?

---

53   De Man, p111.

The Intellectual Part:

Saturnine, The Lesser Infortune *and Forms of Engagement*

> 'Yet I had gone into the army, if I had gone into it for any conscious reason, in order to immerse myself in *la condition humaine*....I entertained some notion that it was my duty as a poet to live through the extremes of contemporary existence.'[54]

Circumstances obliged Heppenstall to abandon his pacifism, the only intellectual stance he had adopted after his Catholicism lapsed. Conscripted in December 1940, he served in the Royal Artillery and the Pay Corps in Yorkshire and Northern Ireland leaving the service in April 1945. After leaving the Army, Heppenstall discovered that it was impossible to live as a 'professional, free-lance writer', as before.[55] He became a producer for BBC Radio's Third Programme, and his creativity was often channelled into broadcasting, but his position ensured that he could remain aware of developments within literary culture, despite curbing his actual output.

After *Sebastian*, he published just twenty short poems, mostly in *Blind Men's Flowers are Green* (1940). These, mostly, retained the lyrical style and religious tone of his thirties work. 'The Planets' importantly introduced an astrological interest that would punctuate Heppenstall's later writing, whilst 'Uneasy Time' suggested that the agnosticism of his earlier poetry had dissolved into spiritual emptiness:

> Particles of dead thought
> Stir all day and find

---

54 Heppenstall, *The Lesser Infortune* (Jonathan Cape: London 1953), p36.

55 *Intellectual Part*, p50.

No means to be used as they ought
On the floor of the mind.[56]

Rayner ultimately rejected Catholic doctrine, admitting, 'I could not manage the omniscience and omnipotence of God, which are pretty basic', and this intellectual-spiritual vacancy coloured his subsequent fiction.[57] Perhaps this informed his decision in 1946 to abandon poetry: the spiritual basis upon which he had structured his verse had collapsed. He continued his journalism, and issued a critical volume, *The Double Image* (1947), examining Christian mythology in four French Catholic writers: Bernanos, Mauriac, Claudel and Léon Bloy, on whom he subsequently produced a monograph.

After *The Blaze of Noon*, Heppenstall originally 'did not intend to write any further novels'.[58] However, its unanticipated *succès d'estime* led him to further explore its possibilities, although he published just two more between 1939 and 1962. Both incorporated Heppenstall's war experiences, confronting the massive challenge of engaging with the hostilities and the immediate post-war upheavals whilst they occurred. *Saturnine* (1943) introduced an anti-hero, Alick Frobisher, living in London during the months surrounding the conflict's opening. In many ways, Frobisher's circumstances mirrored Heppenstall's, but Rayner consciously believed that 'Every piece of writing is a dramatisation', and this was reflected in *Saturnine*'s construction, in which a 'realistic' account of London life (drawn from Heppenstall's own), encompassing bankruptcy, illness, collapsing buildings, literary production, homosexual acquaintances and military service is continually punctuated by fantastical interludes, self-

---

56   Heppenstall, 'Uneasy Time' in *Poems 1933-1945*, p11.

57   *Intellectual Part*, p29.

58   *Blaze of Noon,* p6.

reflection or metafictional ruminations.[59] Only 1,650 copies were published, partly because of paper shortages, but also because its contents were considered inflammatory: publishers were less inclined to gamble on potentially unprofitable ventures, particularly those risking political censure. Unpublished until 1953 but mostly written during Heppenstall's service, *The Lesser Infortune* was a more directly autobiographical novel about Frobisher's military service in England and Ireland, during which he suffers a mental breakdown.

Following developments in French literature, Rayner engaged with two main currents, ideologically and aesthetically opposed: one affiliated to *La Resistance* (comprising Sartre, Camus and Malraux) and the other (to an extent) supporting the Vichy government. Sartre's conceptualisation of *littérature engagée*, underpinned by his Marxist convictions and not antagonistic towards Socialist Realism, emerged from active opposition to the German occupation. However, several of Heppenstall's favourite French writers, particularly Céline, Jouhandeau and Drieu la Rochelle, betrayed sympathies with Nazism.[60]

Saturnine expressed an aspiration to find an alternate reality, away from the war and its competing doctrines. Like *The Blaze of Noon*, it was told in the first person, and this device, while providing a centre which successfully anchors numerous sub-plots and intellectual asides, allowed Heppenstall to continue his investigation into the effects of Modernity upon the sensitive, cultured individual. However, Alick is psychologically more fragile than Louis Dunkel (not having had to overcome disability in the same way), and his eventual breakdown could be read as representative of the disintegration of the (bohemian) bourgeoisie – again, its protagonist

59   Heppenstall, *The Double Image* (Secker & Warburg: London 1947), p66.

60   In fact, Heppenstall's sympathies with Drieu la Rochelle coloured his retrospective opinions on the conflict. There is a bold defence of Drieu in *The Intellectual Part,* p40.

and his associates were definitely middle-class. His insecurity leads him to seek identification with numerous *ideas*, although not with contemporary ideologies. It becomes clear that two objects exert considerable power over his consciousness: the planet Saturn, which he believes inescapable, and his friend Richard St. Hilda, with whom he forms an intensely complex psychological relationship.

The extent of Richard's hold is detailed in a passage that also exemplifies the way in which contemplation of politics becomes intertwined with psychological reflection, which again belies a strong interest in, and lengthy reflection upon Freudian ideas: 'it is one of the elementary facts of existence that no man willingly contains a devil. He will try to exteriorise and as it were incarnate it. Thus the German race has tried to incarnate its devil in the Jews....In the same way, I tried to incarnate my devil in Richard St. Hilda.'[61] Alick, in moments of insecurity, often compares himself to the wealthy and popular Richard, who 'had...looked at a great many philosophical works and still hoped that one day he would find...a simple formula which contained the whole truth....I preferred the muddled earnestness of those who attended the Institute of Mystical Science.'[62] On this issue, Alick initially feels inferior to Richard, whose quest for (and belief in) this philosophical 'formula' seems to him more valid (that is, *scientific*) than the alternative realities he experiments with, but eventually he decides that mysticism and astrology are no more ineffectual than post-Enlightenment thought as a remedy for his malaise.

This 'muddled earnestness' summarises *Saturnine*'s revolt against reason perfectly. It contradicted Sartre's maxim that 'the empire of signs is prose: poetry is on the side of painting, sculpture and music.'[63] This maxim was echoed, curiously enough, in *The Double Image*: 'Prose fiction

---

61   Heppenstall, *Saturnine* (Secker & Warburg: London 1943), p18.

62   Ibid, p35.

63   Jean-Paul Sartre, *What is Literature?* (Harper & Row: New York 1965), p5.

is able to create the possibility of new situations among existing human beings, whereas lyrical poetry can at best emphasise favourite situations among those already established.'[64] *Saturnine*'s prose, however, was deftly lyrical: the 'commitment' its narrative demonstrated was not to political mobilisation, but to seemingly antiquated, irrational belief systems, and even this constantly expired. The 'possibility of new situations', however, was key: the explicit aim of *Saturnine*, and *The Lesser Infortune*, was to 're-produce...the wealth and complexity of the world of the psyche.'[65]

Above all, Heppenstall was committed to *writing*. For the *nouveau roman* authors, 'conscious experimentation with literary form is *in itself* a kind of political engagement', as formal radicalism had become inextricably politicised during the thirties, after the Nazi book burning and Zhdanov's imposition of Socialist Realism. It was perhaps inevitable, given the enormity of the conflict and his own ideological scepticism, that Heppenstall would not attempt 'war novels' that aspired to capture the reality of active conflict in any sense. Both novels concentrated on Frobisher's battle to stay sane with his personal life, and the society he exists within, collapsing around him. It is the day the Blitz begins that makes the war 'real' for Frobisher, making it more than a distant threat that colours his mood: he states that, 'The date on which the old world came to an end was Saturday, September the 7th, 1940.'[66] This inaugurates *The Lesser Infortune*; in *Saturnine*, the threat posed by the political backdrop is accentuated by the sparseness of its intrusion. Often just a brief sentence or paragraph is dropped between different strands of Frobisher's narrative: 'Day by day, the news of Effie's wireless became more heavy with foreboding. The wicked sailor informed us that two German submarines had appeared in

---

64   *Double Image,* p124.

65   Nathalie Sarraute, 'The Age of Suspicion' in *Tropisms and The Age of Suspicion* (John Calder: London 1963), p91.

66   *Lesser Infortune*, p9.

the Medway.'[67]

However, in some ways, the war provides a release for Frobisher, desperate to experience contemporary reality at its most extreme: impulsively, he writes to a friend declaring, 'I am inclined to welcome the prospect of war....Destitution is worse than war, and, for some, war is a remedy against destitution.'[68] During *The Lesser Infortune*, Frobisher's desperation to experience the 'extremes of contemporary reality' costs him his sanity, and this ideologically unclassifiable, implied anti-war 'lesson' is the only comment on the cataclysmic consequences of modernity that can be inferred from the *events* of his narrative – a lesson which Frobisher's insanity prevents him from explicitly recording.

Rayner commented that *Saturnine* 'did not get much of a press, although once more a voice was raised demanding that it should be suppressed.'[69] This was novelist and critic James Agate, who resented a passage reading, 'Consider merely that everyone stinks of excrement and putrefaction. That goes for you and me, for the Prime Minister and the Hangman, for the Queen of England, the little princesses and the Queen Mother, for all the war-lords of Europe.'[70] This opinion, although not expressed by Frobisher (whom critics, not entirely inaccurately, assumed to *be* Heppenstall), caused minor outrage, epitomizing as it did *Saturnine*'s disdain not just for politics but also for *politicians* – a controversial stance that would inevitably offend at a time when unequivocal support for Churchill's National Government was demanded.

Heppenstall did not treat Agate's fury remotely seriously, although after *The Blaze of Noon* he was disappointed that his apoplexy did not boost his sales or critical interest. In *The Lesser Infortune*, this incident is relayed

---

67   *Saturnine*, p33.

68   Ibid, p59.

69   *Intellectual Part*, p46.

70   *Saturnine*, p52.

in an amusing combination of Heppenstall's life story and literary fiction, made possible as both novels are presented as volumes of Frobisher's autobiography: '*Saturnine* was now out. The critics seemed puzzled, by and large. James Agate, however, insisted vehemently that so wicked a book should never have been allowed to appear'. This is followed by a hilarious passage where Frobisher explains how *Saturnine* affected his Army life 'in a number of ways relevant to this narrative.'[71] Unlike *Saturnine*, whose narrative seamlessly jumped between 'reality' and fantastical episodes, *The Lesser Infortune* seemed an attempt by Heppenstall to disprove his own belief that it was impossible to 'present the reality of a man's life', as B. S. Johnson always insisted an author should.[72] Heppenstall's memoirs and journals reveal that the major characters in *The Lesser Infortune* were based on his acquaintances (its 'Dorian Scott-Crichton' was fellow novelist Julian MacLaren-Ross, for example), drawn from Heppenstall's wartime 'reality'.

This 'reality' was immensely problematic, given the all-encompassing nature of the hostilities, with numerous unprecedented implications for civilians worldwide. Frobisher's mental instability, which leads to him, like Heppenstall, failing to leave Britain and being removed from service before the fall of Berlin, makes apprehending this fragmentary 'reality' even more difficult. Aware of this uncertainness of this 'reality' (and its intangible, fragile nature was what rendered it worthy of fictionalisation), Frobisher eventually becomes unable to trust any information, saying 'I'm afraid', I said, 'that I feel about this war as some people feel about God. I keep wondering if it really exists.'[73] Realising the futility of trying to present Frobisher's life as 'reality' for anyone except himself, Heppenstall simply lends his protagonist his own experience of barracks and mental

---

71   *Lesser Infortune*, pp217-218.

72   *Double Image*, p70.

73   *Lesser Infortune*, p262.

institutions, and has him record them as faithfully as possible.

This characterisation of Frobisher, as an author writing an autobiographical text, and explicitly reflecting on this process, can be understood through Barthes' later distinction between *figuration*, in which 'the author may appear in his text...but not in the guise of direct biography', and *representation*, in which the author *did* appear in the text, *as himself*.[74] Heppenstall's metafictional self-consciousness allowed him to contravene this differentiation: he does not *actually* appear in the text as himself, but wittily attributes *Saturnine* to Frobisher (a *figuration* who *represents* Heppenstall's literary career) avoiding the necessity of Heppenstall intruding upon a text that hitherto has not included him, as Johnson did in *Christie Malry's Own Double Entry*. Often, this metafictional structure provided an outlet for his (now familiar) dry, ironic humour, drawing its comedic value from the assumptions that can be drawn about *Saturnine*'s impact on Heppenstall's personal life: Frobisher recounts that another consequence of publishing *Saturnine* was that Tessa Duveen, Nathalie Fröhlich and Pat Mallard (three of its characters) 'had all purchased firearms.'[75]

The concentration upon Frobisher's 'I', ignoring any organisation or community, in itself made Heppenstall's novels unusual within contemporary British writing on World War Two. However, this was far from unusual within literary history, as numerous genres incorporated the use of a first-person narrative into their stylistic traditions. Rayner revived the antiquated term 'picaresque' to describe *Saturnine*, explaining: 'The essence of a *picaresque* novel is...that it is told in the first person by a social parasite, rogue, picaroon or (as we say now) anti-hero and...that it has no formal plot but that the episodes simply follow each other serially.'[76] This genre suited him as he could post these episodes to an acquaintance

---

74   Roland Barthes, *The Pleasure of the Text* (Jonathan Cape: London 1975), p56.

75   *Lesser Infortune*, p218.

76   *Intellectual Part*, p46.

as he wrote them, creating it without any preliminary scheme, or even pre-determined plot. Later, when *Saturnine* was revised and reissued as *The Greater Infortune*, Heppenstall regretted that readers 'took both *Saturnine* and *The Lesser Infortune* to be more autobiographical than they are and formed (while one or two critics expressed) conclusions unflattering to myself. They forgot that it is the essence of *picaresque* fiction to represent itself as autobiography and to be ostensibly the work of a social parasite, rogue or picaroon.'[77]

Derrida stated that 'Every text *participates* in one or several genres', and *Saturnine*, like Robbe-Grillet's *The Erasers*, extended its genre's boundaries and subverted the formal expectations associated with it.[78] One of *Saturnine*'s most fascinating moments comes when the text displays awareness of its own fragmented nature, and its own difficulty in sewing together its divergent strands into any structure, and deliberately attacks itself. 'It seems as if I were telling four or five stories at once, but that is how it was. I can imagine this story divided up between four or five distinct novels.' These would, Frobisher explains, be novels about the revenge of Alick's suppressed romanticism after his bankruptcy, decadent intellectual life in pre-war London and 'the disintegration of personality remedied by a national Risorgimento,' and a simpler novel about Alick's child being born, but 'More interesting...would be a highly atmospheric novel dealing with experiences in a half-world of death and rebirth.' However, the complexity of the interaction between these stories, loosely but effectively linked by their narrator, means that Alick is unable to (and does not *have* to) explicate them. He acknowledges that the resultant narrative is chaotic, conceding: 'Any attempt at all-embracing consistency would be dishonest (and I believe that it is always so in life and that all novel-writing is dishonest in its degree). I can but play upon the surface and hint at underly-

---

77   Heppenstall, *The Greater Infortune* (Peter Owen: London 1960), p5.

78   Jacques Derrida, 'The Law of Genre' in *Acts of Literature* (Routledge: New York/London 1992), p230.

ing depths wherever I am aware of them.'[79] Unlike Louis in *The Blaze of Noon*, who regrets *losing* control of his story, Frobisher admits that he *never* controlled it, confessing, 'I cannot truthfully say what effect attached to what cause or indeed which was cause and which effect' — any attempt at consistency would fail as his own life story is too complicated. Crucially, though, his deconstruction of his narrative does not undermine his own centrality: his story always picks itself up after such moments when its narrator questions its form.

Robbe-Grillet believed that narrative technicalities 'impose the image of a stable, coherent, continuous, unequivocal, entirely decipherable universe.'[80] In *Saturnine*'s text, no attempt to impose this image is ever made; the novel revels in its own disjointedness, and although most of its fantastical occurrences (such as Alick's 'death' and subsequent near-death experience) can be, and eventually are explained, there is one interlude that remains a puzzle. Richard St. Hilda, Alick's crucial Other, shrinks visibly before him; struggling to remain calm, Alick attempts to lift him, but 'Immediately, he dropped away to a powder so fine that my gasp of astonishment scattered him widely over the room, and he was no longer distinguishable from the motes of dust.'[81] Is this a dream? Or a fantasy? Given Richard's psychological hold over Alick, this would not seem unremarkable, but neither clarification is offered for this scene, which defies all explanation — a defiance that feels aesthetically congruous with the narrative framing it, encapsulating Frobisher's rejection of post-Enlightenment philosophy in an unexplainable moment. In the next scene, Frobisher visits a priest, but shies away from discussing this 'death', and it is never mentioned again. Soon, St. Hilda returns to the narrative, eventually dying towards the end of the war, and the trauma remains beyond ratio-

---

79   *Saturnine*, p93.

80   Robbe-Grillet, 'On Several Obsolete Notions', p32.

81   *Saturnine*, p69.

nalisation. Richard's 'actual' death (from an unspecified but not unusual illness) occurs near the end of *The Lesser Infortune*, the banality of which is recorded with genuine sobriety: 'A rubber tube connected to the tap terminated in a short length of glass tube, and this had been inserted into Richard's arm. The apparatus was, it seemed, a glucose dripper, by means of which Richard had to be nourished until he could again feed through the stomach.'[82] He dies soon after.

Frobisher, too, 'dies' in *Saturnine*, hit by a falling tile – he earlier survives the ceiling falling at Marginal Road, which, he recalls with an entertaining combination of accuracy and ambivalence, happens on 'Sunday morning, the 8th or 15th of January, 1939.'[83] Obviously, he remains alive at the end of *The Lesser Infortune*: this is swiftly revealed as the catalyst for a near-death experience, as Alick recounts, 'I began to wish that I had not died....I did not know how long I had been away, but perhaps on earth they had not yet buried my physical body....I wondered how best to put this matter to the Guardian of the Threshold.'[84] After a frank, hilarious discussion with the Guardian about memory and his attempt to abolish his past, the Freudian 'death-wish' (dismissed as a 'misleading' buzzword), reincarnation and the search for 'peace', Frobisher is returned to his body, and his narrative survives his own 'death'.

Barthes declared that, 'The text needs its shadow: this shadow is a *bit* of ideology, a *bit* of representation, a *bit* of a subject.'[85] It is the *possibility* of this death that permeates both novels, given the symbolic and actual death that war threatens. It colours Heppenstall's investigation into Frobisher's psychological collapse, as the conflict becomes, for him, an intolerable procession of inflexible officers, insensitive soldiers and intellectual depri-

---

82   *Lesser Infortune*, p250.

83   *Saturnine*, p15.

84   Ibid, p121.

85   Barthes, *Pleasure*, p32.

vation. This instability, exacerbated by barrack conditions, springs primarily from Alick's belief that his deeply ingrained introspectiveness ought to give over to an assumption of collective responsibility, which demands fundamental, impossible changes to his personality: 'But I must not go on thinking, 'I...I...I...' That way lay madness. 'I' must be only the shadow and the recorder. The sensitive, recording mind could remain (I hoped). The sensitive ego, the life sensitive to its own impulses and motions, must certainly disappear.'[86] It does not, and cannot – the incessant wireless broadcasts, artificial light and a coarse roommate drive the relentlessly analytical Frobisher to insanity.

This breakdown appears solemn and dignified – Frobisher sinks into a quiet, highly introverted clinical depression. Consequently, Alick's opinions about the pointlessness of existing when all 'causes' to which he could devote himself have become implicated in the ongoing atrocities, in which he now actively participates, do not change, but his manner of expressing them does. In *Saturnine*, this hopelessness is manifested in gleeful, subversive humour, a stylistic flourish often associated with the *picaresque* genre. 'I developed a phantasy. I thought that henceforward I would go through the world with a rope about my neck....If anybody were...to ask me about it, I would explain that I was herein expressing my true condition.'[87] In *The Lesser Infortune*, this extravagant social commentary dissolves into existential despair: its far less colourful prose is closer to Camus or Blanchot, and while it never feels incongruous as a continuation of *Saturnine*, the earlier novel's strident textual exuberance is notably absent.

The Lesser Infortune was less obviously *picaresque*, more a (seemingly) conventional first-person account of Army life. Joining the Army necessarily terminates many strands of *Saturnine*'s narrative, centring the plot in one location, offering a much smaller (and generally less diverse) cast,

---

86   *Lesser Infortune*, p37.

87   *Saturnine*, pp39-40.

and the impact of this loss of freedom upon Frobisher's consciousness is significant. Alick explains, 'I felt, indeed, that this army was a widely scattered system of concentration camps designed to immobilise the more potentially active and independent part of the population while the present disorders subsisted.'[88] *The Lesser Infortune*'s absence of the multi-directional structure of *Saturnine* reflects Frobisher's lack of psychological freedom, with its comparative formal restraint being appropriate to, and determined by, its sombre content. However, its relentless depiction of the material world, integrating moments of intellectual analysis into lengthy object description, provided aesthetic continuity with *The Blaze of Noon* and anticipated Robbe-Grillet's observatory style. The novel opens with a long representational passage: 'Two lines intersect at Tottenham Rivers, and for this reason the station has an importance disproportionate to its size. Or rather the two stations, for there is a high-level halt about a quarter of a mile up the hill, on the edge of the forest.'[89] The quiet, casual tone of this writing recalled the poetic voice-overs that often featured in British documentaries, and particularly those of Humphrey Jennings, the Surrealist poet turned filmmaker. However, it is punctuated by personal reflection, which constantly reminds the reader that the novel is conducting an investigation into Frobisher's state of consciousness, again moving the descriptive writing into an area beyond the representational reach of the camera.

These observations inevitably differed from those of *The Blaze of Noon* as the narrator possesses sight, but certainty about the external world has been destabilised by Frobisher's breakdown, an ailment seemingly harder to compensate for than blindness. An aside such as, 'The five men immediately to my left are political desperadoes. Shabbily dressed, they nevertheless betray a certain care for effect. Two of them are more in need of a shave than I am, but the features of all are fine. This is what

---

88   *Lesser Infortune*, p46.

89   Ibid, p7.

makes me certain', is typical of the narrator's detached style, in which the exterior world is meticulously observed, analysed and then related back to himself, often with the dry humour and façade of analytical certainty of Heppenstall's debut novel.[90] The otherworldly possibilities explored in *Saturnine* are not discounted entirely, although they are discussed in far more sober tones: Alick describes a dream in which 'I was sitting in a signal-box. There appeared to be neither material nor spiritual logic in this. A signal-box had never been one of my dream-symbols…The supposition that this might be an echo from a previous life was untenable. According to the best information, a man rarely becomes incarnate more than once in two thousand years'; although here, the idea that he may have inherited dream symbols from a past life is rejected, the concept of reincarnation is not.[91]

The prose that concludes *The Lesser Infortune* is, in my opinion, the strongest in any of Heppenstall's fiction. The end of the war is relayed in an astonishingly understated, almost indifferent style, in a manner that is frank and deeply personal, whilst remaining conscious of the political problems it both resolves and creates. The single paragraph capturing the brief historical moment between the realisation of an Allied victory and the collapse of fascism is sublime: the minimal extent to which the war has previously impacted upon the text lends it tremendous strength, as it finally betrays Alick's feelings about the wider conflict framing his introspective tale. It follows Alick's demobilisation (when he declares a life-long history of mental illness under pressure from his medical orderly) and comes between his reflection on his dreams, featuring the departed St. Hilda, and his future beyond his last day at Tottenham Rivers. The gravity of its subject lends it a climactic feel, as if it is the moment towards

---

90   Ibid, p14.

91   Ibid, p16.

which Heppenstall's consistently delicate stylisation has been ascending: 'History's supernumeraries, Hitler and Mussolini, were still alive. The beauties of Buchenwald and Belsen remained, for the moment, unrevealed. In France, there was widespread embarrassment. Not everybody had behaved in a manner now likely to meet with public approval. The Spanish Government realised that it had backed the wrong horse and made haste to sever diplomatic relations with the Japanese, whose troubles were only just beginning.'[92] Frobisher is unable to welcome the close of the war as he did its opening: he finds that he has merely traded his participation in the collective uncertainty about the future of the world for an isolated uncertainty about his own, in a society which he can no longer understand. He concludes: 'I breathed deeply of the magical air and came back into myself. I would look no further than that small house in a narrow lane.'[93] He returns to a location from his pre-war existence, but that location is all that remains.

Saturnine and *The Lesser Infortune* were unique within the corpus of writing that arose in response to the war, either during it or its immediate aftermath. Even if it was Heppenstall's friend Orwell who produced the most prescient novels about the post-war political situation, Heppenstall's investigations into the relationship between the individual and the consummate crisis of modernity were equally indicative of the untenable position of 'rational' belief systems: he recognised the war as 'the end of recourse to Freudian, Marxist or Christian alibis.'[94] They are as representative, in their (far more introspective) way, of their time as Orwell's novels, and a valuable contribution to the project of establishing new literary conventions and issues for exploration after those central to (late) Modernist writing became untenable.

---

92   Ibid, p272.

93   Ibid.

94   *Intellectual Part*, p62.

Curiously, when critics *have* addressed Heppenstall, these novels have virtually always been ignored, not just because they so completely defied all expectations of war literature, but also because of the unfortunate circumstances regarding their publication. *Saturnine* was promised a reprint, but this was never fulfilled, and so it did not reappear until Heppenstall published *The Greater Infortune*, incorporating a chapter from its sequel and changing Frobisher's name to Leckie, a redraft which, curiously, lost something of *Saturnine*'s magical, extravagant chaos. A revision of *The Lesser Infortune*, intended for simultaneous publication, went unreleased as the novel was technically still in print with Jonathan Cape, who did little to promote the book on its original release. Nonetheless, it remains surprising that in their brief asides on Heppenstall, John Carey, Hélène Cixous and Randall Stevenson all neglect these works, which have rarely (if ever) been featured in discussions about British war literature.

The only exception has been Julian Symons, who felt that 'There is nothing else like *Saturnine*'s mixture of philosophical reflection, near-mysticism, triviality and fact in modern literature, and [it]...is surely Heppenstall's most considerable achievement.'[95] Indeed, every episode of *Saturnine* is fascinating, both in itself and (particularly) within the context of the narrative's rich, disorderly tapestry, and its playful approach to the *picaresque* form, idiosyncratic intellectualising and acidic wit make it the most pleasurable of Heppenstall's novels. Moreover, its metatextuality and its post-Surrealist focus upon astrology and 'irrational' states of consciousness prefigured strands within French (more than British) literature: particularly *The Planetarium* by Sarraute and Robbe-Grillet's use of tarot cards, but also the writings of some of the (less politically-minded) fringe members of the Lettrist group, such as those of keen astrologer and poet Jean-Louis Brau.

---

95   Symons, p20.

On *The Lesser Infortune*, both Symons and its author were less enthusiastic. Heppenstall stated that it received lukewarm reviews, and 'I myself was discontented with it.'[96] Symons concluded that, while it was not without interest, the novel 'certainly bears no relation to [Heppenstall's] developing theories of fiction.'[97] This does the novel a major disservice. It was abortively assembled whilst Rayner was on service, and most of its episodes were written before 1945, with some published in contemporary periodicals. Whatever his 'theories' were at this point, Heppenstall later stated his belief that certain passages, 'Elaborated only a little further...might well have been found in...something like Robbe-Grillet's *Instantanés*.'[98] Its observatory style and fixation upon an internal consciousness that rejected the possibility of an objective 'reality' anticipated fundamental characteristics in Robbe-Grillet and Sarraute, both establishing themselves as important (anti-)novelists when *The Lesser Infortune* appeared.

After *The Lesser Infortune*, Heppenstall concentrated on his broadcasting, while closely following developments within British and French literature – both the 'Angry Young Men' and the *nouveau roman*, towards which the Young Men became increasingly hostile. He did not publish another novel for nine years, by which time his 'developing theories of fiction' would be radically influenced by one novel in particular – Robbe-Grillet's *Jealousy*.

---

96   *Intellectual Part*, p192.

97   Symons, p20.

98   *Intellectual Part*, p212.

A Continuing Present:

The Connecting Door, The Woodshed *and* *'Experimental' Literature*

> 'The *nouveau roman* had given me courage...I felt able,
> without misgiving, to do what I had long wanted to do.'[99]

For the latter half of the fifties, Heppenstall, occupied with the BBC, published nothing. Even considering the sporadic nature of his previous literary output, this represented a lengthy hiatus: he re-emerged with a flurry of creativity at the turn of the decade, issuing two novels, two volumes of memoirs and a critical work. *Four Absentees* appeared first, in 1960. Heppenstall's candid reminiscences about his friends Orwell, Dylan Thomas and Eric Gill infuriated several publications, which deified these figures (those on Middleton Murry sparked less outrage). For some critics, Heppenstall's revelations confirmed their suspicions about *his* character. Its retrospective focus on 'absentees' was telling, suggesting that Heppenstall was conscious that a phase in his literary career had ended, and that he sought a new direction.

Heppenstall's next publication, *The Fourfold Tradition* (1961), was an ambitious critical work, demonstrating how the Norman imposition of French as the 'official' language had initiated an important relationship between it and English, engendering concurrent 'first' and 'second' traditions in English and French literature. Heppenstall characterised these 'first' traditions as the discourses of formally (and often religiously) conventional literature, from the medieval period to the present. In opposition the 'second' traditions existed, within which there were numerous

---

99   *Intellectual Part*, p210.

sub-traditions, various 'experimental' attempts to explore alternate aesthetic possibilities.

Naturally, Heppenstall expressed a preference for French literature, especially its 'second' tradition. He was particularly interested in the related 'stream-of-consciousness' and 'inner monologue' techniques, which, he claimed, originated with Dujardin in France and were simultaneously developed by Joyce, Woolf, Lawrence, Gide, Proust and Jouhandeau. In England, this had become 'bedevilled with literary politics', as the 'Angry Young Men', whom Heppenstall portrayed as parochial (despite stating elsewhere that he had enjoyed Kingsley Amis' *Lucky Jim*), violently opposed its use.[100]

Across the Channel, this tradition had culminated in the *nouveau roman*, which Heppenstall considered 'more stimulating than anything... at present' in English literature, and an interesting variant on stream-of-consciousness' writing.[101] He viewed the determination of 'an influential group of novelists', infuriated by Robbe-Grillet's (translated) *Le Voyeur*, to 'run experimental writing out of town' with amused disdain; he had never advocated anything so passionately as the 'anti-novel'.[102] He met Michel Butor, Marguerite Duras and Nathalie Sarraute, who praised *The Greater Infortune*, as well as Alain Robbe-Grillet, before the London premiere of *L'Année dernière à Marienbad*, scripted by Robbe-Grillet and directed by Alain Resnais. Discussing their reviews (uppermost in Heppenstall's mind after *Four Absentees*), Robbe-Grillet remarked that his career had 'been based entirely upon the acreage of insulting comment' passed on his work.[103]

At the time, Heppenstall was writing two novels, which, again, formed one continuous narrative, although unlike *Saturnine* and *The Lesser Infortune*, it was not chronologically linear. These were *The Connecting Door* and *The*

---

100   *Fourfold Tradition*, p142.

101   Ibid, p270.

102   *Intellectual Part*, p198.

103   Ibid, p209.

Woodshed, both published in 1962. Several reviewers, interested in British attempts to produce a domestic 'anti-novel', seized upon the publisher's label for the former, and compared Heppenstall to Robbe-Grillet. Rayner admitted that 'especially to a lapsed poet, the [*nouveau roman*] was very attractive, with its tightly formal structure, its spaced repetition of certain themes [and]...its classical regard for one or another set of unities', although he conceded that Robbe-Grillet would have considered *The Connecting Door* an imperfect practice of his doctrine.[104] Its narrative concerned a journalist on an assignment at the Franco-German border in 1948, and his relations with two men (Harold and Atha), two women (Annalies and Madame Zix), several other characters and the landscape.

The Woodshed never claimed to be an anti-novel; rather, it was a practical attempt by Heppenstall to separate the 'stream-of-consciousness' technique from 'literary politics', hoping that it could once again be 'judged on its merits', as he felt it had before the war.[105] This was Heppenstall's engagement with England's 'second tradition': it began with Harold Atha on a train, travelling from Aberystwyth to his hometown of Hinderholme, Yorkshire, after receiving a telegram stating that his father is dying, prompting much reflection on his childhood.

Despite sharing their central character, the two novels formally differed greatly, far more than *Saturnine* and *The Lesser Infortune*. In *The Connecting Door*, Heppenstall's structural experimentation was more conspicuous, and more strident than ever before; he had closely followed the development of the *nouveau roman*, which 'increasingly [took] the form of a foregrounding of the structural as opposed to the representational aspects of the text' during the sixties.[106] Unlike in *Jealousy*, *The Connecting Door*'s central 'I' *does* act in his story, making Heppenstall's assault upon the conventions of first-person narrative less radical than Robbe-Grillet's.

---

104   Ibid, p199.

105   *Fourfold Tradition*, p142.

106   Britton, p49.

This 'I' spends much of his time meticulously recording details about his surroundings in a notebook, highlighting the process of writing. That this nameless 'I' will centre this process is established by Heppenstall's first sentence, which becomes a textual motif: 'At whatever time I awake, bells are ringing.'[107] On their first appearance, the bells prompt lengthy description of the narrator's surroundings, in his hotel and in the town. While this opening passage details his relationship not just with his space but those who inhabit it, the narrator attempts to maintain neutrality, aiming to avoid the 'pathetic fallacy' which allowed objects 'to act with a personal force'.[108]

At first glance, it seems that the narrator is constructing his text so as to render this possible. Object observation is not often intertwined with intellectual analysis in Heppenstall's usual fashion. He had assimilated Robbe-Grillet's idea that objects should 'be *there* before being something' and 'still be there afterwards...eternally present, mocking their own 'meaning', and *The Connecting Door*'s descriptions *appear* more neutral than those of *The Lesser Infortune*.[109] Adjectives are utilised sparingly, usually describing nothing beyond an object's physical properties – the text rarely states the narrator's opinions on exterior objects, ideas or characters, which contrast markedly with Heppenstall's previous narrative style.

However, given Atha's temporal and spatial location, little of the external world can remain free of historical or ideological association. The narrator seldom highlights their significance, maintaining his prosaic, 'objective' style throughout. Passages regarding sites of political meaning simply describe their physical features, usually without stating a position on the atrocities that generated their significance; where value judgements are inserted into the text, they never directly concern politics. For ex-

---

107   Heppenstall, *The Connecting Door* (Barrie & Rockliff: London 1962), p9.

108   *Fourfold Tradition*, p191.

109   Robbe-Grillet, 'A Future for the Novel', p21.

ample, walking along a pathway, the narrator notes that 'the first thing you see is a rough-hewn slab of pink stone, polished on one side and bearing the names of nine men...who were murdered at this point and their bodies thrown into the Rhine by the Gestapo in flight, in November 1944, three and a half years ago.'[110] His very decision to note this 'unimpressive monument', and particularly its inscription, itself constitutes an implicit political statement, and it becomes apparent that the novel's prominent structural features deliberately mask its fundamental investigations. Firstly, its façade of journalistic objectivity disguises an immensely subjective novel, querying the position of the 'I', not the nature of the society he visits, and in which political significance of objects remains subservient to personal significance (as in the novels of Claude Simon or Duras). Secondly, the textual awareness of space hides the fact that the novel is primarily concerned with time.

To be precise, *The Connecting Door* is concerned with *memory*, inextricably linked with time; the function of its space is to trigger these memories and consequently the interaction between the 'I', Harold, and Atha. Like many other *nouveau roman* works, Heppenstall's novel 'creates its own temporal series as it goes along.'[111] Its events occur in 1931, 1936 and 1948, on separate trips to mainland Europe; that its central figure simultaneously exists across these three planes of time, as three distinct characters, only gradually becomes apparent. The novel presents a series of clues that the 'I', 'Harold' and 'Atha' are in fact one person, with their 'interaction' taking place entirely within Harold Atha's consciousness. Having already introduced the younger versions of himself, the narrator explains that 'the age of fairly-young Atha (the pseudo-Atha, as I begin to think of him to myself) is in fact twenty-four. He is thus five years older than Harold and

---

110   *Connecting Door*, p37.

111   Sturrock, p25.

twelve years younger than me.'[112]

In order to allow Harold Atha this temporal multiplicity, Heppenstall had to be creative in his use of tense. Events in 1931 or 1936 are recorded in the same present tense as those in 1948 (and, finally, 1949), leaving the reader to establish which events are taking place in the present and which in the past, and which conversations occur in 'reality' (and *which* 'reality') and which in Atha's imagination. That 'the present' is 1948 is established through statements such as 'The Russians are being trouble-some to the British and the Americans both in Berlin and in Vienna. In London, the future of the Rhine is under discussion', which locate Atha's narrative at a very specific historical moment.[113] Incongruous temporal signifiers intrude upon this narrative with increasing frequency, seemingly integrated perfectly into what appears to be 'the present'. A section on Atha's trip to Kehl jumps between 1936 and 1948, and it becomes clear that the Kehl that 'Atha' sees is one that the narrator remembers from his last visit: 'the main street had been renamed the Adolf-Hitlerstrasse. In the shop windows, swastika-stamped notices assured indifferent Atha that business there was conducted wholly by and with Aryans.'[114] Harold Atha's memories of the 1936 visit assume the form of an external charac-ter, possessing the ability to reproach Atha for his actions and inactions, and for compromising his previously deeply held beliefs.

If Robbe-Grillet was the dominant influence upon *The Connecting Door*'s textual style and structural ambiguity, Sarraute's ideas informed Heppenstall's characterisation. Sarraute maintained that readers no longer trusted 'characters' in novels, aware that they were often thinly drawn personifications of conflicting aspects of the writer's personality,

---

112   *Connecting Door*, p46.

113   Ibid, p17.

114   Ibid, p65.

or sketches of their acquaintances.[115] Heppenstall decided against trying to create credible individuals. Aware that major characters could only be constructed from the author's consciousness, he deliberately split his first-person narrator into three subjects, a device which replaced the narrator's self-interrogation that Rayner previously favoured. Indeed, Atha's centrality is never questioned, either here or in *The Woodshed*. Heppenstall combined this with Sarraute's focus on 'inner dramas of the *present* moment' – such dramas constitute *The Connecting Door*'s scenes of confrontation.[116] The 'I', 'Harold' and 'Atha' 'meet' in several places, but their increasingly chimerical façade of individuality finally collapses when the narrator encounters 'Harold' at the station. The narrator tells 'Harold', 'There was a war', and his younger self is astonished to hear that the Americans bombed their French allies (and, specifically, the Minster) for strategic reasons.[117] When 'Harold' claims to remember a war (perhaps the Great War), the narrator attacks him, asking what he did yesterday. He then tells 'Harold', 'You were doing nothing...because I didn't think about you. In the past seventeen years, you've lived in occasional flickers, when I had you in mind. You forget, or, rather, you haven't quite realised, that without me you don't exist.'[118]

Barthes stated that fictional writing, and characterisation in particular, involved 'giving the imaginary the formal guarantee of the real'.[119] The great nineteenth-century authors rarely questioned the validity of their personification, creating numerous characters that had attained cultural familiarity, and many Modernist writers also strove to present their central figures as 'real' people, often straining extant formal boundaries in

115   Sarraute, p91.

116   Stephen Heath, *The Nouveau Roman* (Elek: London 1972), p47.

117   *Connecting Door,* p120

118   Ibid, p121.

119   Barthes, *Writing Degree Zero*, p39.

their attempts to construct these characters more convincingly. Having given the products of Atha's imagination this formal guarantee for much of his narrative, Heppenstall deftly engineering its collapse in this climactic scene, removing any possibility of belief in their 'reality'.

Paul de Man noted that 'interpretation is nothing but the possibility of error.'[120] *The Connecting Door* allowed numerous interpretations, challenging its reader to correctly identify its subjects of investigation, its temporal and spatial setting and the key events of its narrative. Heppenstall establishes (and sustains) a tone of ironic ambiguity, one even more striking than in his other literary works, that suggests that its events will defy any single, rational explanation, as on occasions in *Saturnine*. Perhaps, by the end, Heppenstall has not allowed enough room for debate about the identity of 'Harold' and 'Atha' – despite the persistently uncertain tone, Heppenstall's clues have unmistakably revealed that the subject is split. The text's relentless temporal play, however, is what makes an often conventional account of a journalistic assignment intriguing, with the *absence* of the war (which has prevented Atha from revisiting the Rhine until 1948) providing a fascinating shadow behind Atha's complex web of interpersonal relations and self-reflections.

The closing events of the novel promise some reconciliation of imagination and reality, past and present. It is only at this ending, on a final visit in 1949, that the words 'connecting door' become significant, when Atha recognises a woman on a train but cannot determine her identity. During the thirties, Atha has a defining relationship with Annalies (the 'Orangerie girl'), who rejects him to wed a wealthier man; in 1948, the widow Madame Zix impacts upon Atha's consciousness. The woman is one of them, Atha explains: he excludes the possibility that Annalies *is* Madame Zix (with 'Zix' being Annalies' married name) by stating that he has not seen Zix for a year, or Annalies for thirteen. He tells himself, 'It cannot have been, it cannot be, Annalies. And yet the impression persists', and

---

120   De Man, p141.

the narrative terminates as he enters her carriage.[121] However, Heppenstall has hinted earlier in his text that they too are one character – describing Mme. Zix with his usual detachment, the narrator notes, 'Again struck by her resemblance to the 'Orangerie girl'.[122] This signifier permits considerable doubt: it allows the reader to *suspect* that Mme Zix is Annalies, but not to be certain, just as Atha suspects but cannot be certain. Crucially, it also allows Heppenstall to end his novel on a note of fundamental ambiguity. Like *The Blaze of Noon*, *The Connecting Door* emerges as a novel that asks whether any knowledge, however ascertained, can ever be considered reliable (here calling into question the reliability of recognition and sight denied to Louis Dunkel), and concludes that all 'certainties' must be regarded with the highest degree of skepticism. This, implicitly, becomes a comment on writing – it is impossible to produce any meaningful 'conclusion' to a discourse of events, or even an adequate sense of closure. Atha makes this clear, calmly stating, 'That is all. I shall be granted no revelation about the long significance of my life. No imaginative creation will be finished.'[123]

The Woodshed is similarly concerned with time and memory, but structured very differently; Heppenstall clearly meant it as a contribution to England's 'second tradition', rather than as an experiment in transposing developments in French neo-Modernist literature into a British novel. Its present is 1948, between Atha's final Rhineland trips; however, the past that the novel addresses precedes that of *The Connecting Door*, with Atha continually being prompted by external stimuli (be they people, places or objects) to reflect upon a childhood spanning from 1914 to 1927.

That *The Woodshed* also investigates the narrator's memory becomes apparent almost immediately, not hidden here under a deliberately misleading structural framework. Atha knows, before recounting, that the

---

121   *Connecting Door*, p162.

122   Ibid, p111.

123   Ibid, p163.

content of his story will necessitate the 'stream-of-consciousness' form, not unlike Dorothy Richardson's in *Pilgrimage*, and that this narrative will be constructed in a 'deliberate' fashion, despite its attempts to present itself as 'automatic' or spontaneous.[124] His considerations on this are typically sardonic. He explains, in a passage recalling *Saturnine*'s self-deconstruction (although far less exuberant): 'In a train, your consciousness streams like a cold. Mr. A. regrets. Mr. A. is confined to his carriage with a streaming consciousness. If I had a secretary sitting opposite with short-hand notebook, or a dictaphone, I could just talk like this. They reckon about ten thousand words to the hour. In a journey of eight hours, you could finish a book. Change the names, and you'd have a stream-of-consciousness novel. A man travelling somewhere for a purpose. What had led up to it, hopes and fears, retrospect and apprehension mingling, things noted as the landscape slid by. At the end, some kind of pay-off. The fears were groundless, the person was not there or had changed his mind, some accident took place, the person or place no longer existed. Had just died perhaps.'[125]

This apprehension pervades *The Woodshed*, with Atha again speculating on the futility of attempting to pull together his fragmented memories into a structural framework that satisfies conventional literary expectations. He discusses his inability to convincingly do so, stating: 'Odd, how my Rhineland pilgrimages should at once thereafter involve me with my father again. But that is looking for coincidence and pattern. There've only been two such pilgrimages, and this time there is no causal connection... The only conceivable link would be metaphysical.'[126] Atha's anecdotes have a strong centre – the powerful, familiar relationship between the dying father and his son – but any conscious attempt to impose further

---

124   *Fourfold Tradition*, p143.

125   Heppenstall, *The Woodshed* (Jupiter: London 1968), p13.

126   Ibid, p17.

order upon them would be arbitrary. William James' term 'stream-of-consciousness' originally suggested a chronologically linear exploration of intertwined memory and emotions: *The Woodshed*, unlike Heppenstall's pre-sixties novels, dispensed with this coherent temporality, but less radically than in *The Connecting Door* or in some of Robbe-Grillet or Sarraute's novels. As in *The Connecting Door*, Atha's narration continually moved from past to present, but despite this, the past recounted was chronologically ordered: it was punctuated, but ultimately undisturbed, by the sporadic returns of Atha's attention to the present.

Although stylistically further from the *nouveau roman*, Heppenstall's novel embraced Robbe-Grillet's belief that 'Literature simply reveals the situation of man and of the universe with which he is at grips.'[127] Certainly, *The Woodshed* does not strive to explore any 'great' social or political themes. By the sixties, writers again felt able to concentrate solely on literary form without fearing accusations of social irresponsibility. The shadow of war behind *Saturnine* and *The Lesser Infortune*, and (in a far more elliptical manner) *The Connecting Door* had no strong equivalent in *The Woodshed*.

Structurally, *The Woodshed* was far less ambitious than *The Connecting Door*, or indeed any of Heppenstall's previous novels. Despite its occasional time shifts, there is no real temporal experimentation – no attempt to challenge the reader through defamiliarisation of novelistic time, and none of *Saturnine*'s adventurous straining of the narrative in contradictory directions. It reintroduces, however, Heppenstall's use of the central figure to determine signification not just of objects but also of people, often establishing a highly considered metaphorical framework within which they are characterised.[128] Heppenstall's sympathetic presentation of homosexual

---

127   Robbe-Grillet, 'On Several Obsolete Notions', p39.

128   Derrida, 'Force and Signification', p19.

characters in *The Blaze of Noon* and *The Lesser Infortune* here becomes Atha's defining same-sex relationship with a classmate, recounted without suggestion that it was some sort of youthful aberration, or any other moral judgement. Occurring while Atha studies Classics, he attempts to draw parallels between this relationship's personae and the philosophical narrative constructed by Plato in his *Lysis* dialogue. 'In my own mind, I cast as Socrates our amiable, elderly Latin master...it was in his lessons that I normally sat by Peter Holmes and let my hand rest on a warm, smooth knee'.[129] However, this imposition fails as Atha admits that 'The figure conspicuously lacking was any Ctesippus.'[130] This is perhaps the most sustained of *The Woodshed*'s literary in-jokes, wryly satirising Joyce's Homeric construction of *Ulysses*, ultimately demonstrating such parallelism to be deeply contrived, and inapplicable to disorderly 'reality'.

The Woodshed is again a novel about self-definition amidst modernity – for what is youth but an extended process of self-definition? It bears the influence of English-language (rather than French) writing more conspicuously than any of his previous works, particularly that of Joyce's *Portrait of the Artist as a Young Man*. Atha grows up in the age of high modernity: he reads Pound, listens to Schönberg, flirts with Communism and Christianity, and these interests put him at odds with his father, whose perceived simplicity he resents. Atha understands that such interpersonal friction usually has several defining moments, and he is able to select one incident that irreversibly damaged their relationship. Atha's father reacts angrily to his son's demonstration of scientific knowledge, and Atha never quite forgives him, reflecting, 'He may have thought I was showing off. He may have thought that I had got it wrong. He may have been a prey to some private resentment at the time. However it may have been, the harm was done. I was

---

129   *Woodshed*, p111.

130   Ibid.

deeply offended, and I decided that frank communication between us was hopeless.'[131]

As in *The Blaze of Noon*, *The Woodshed* displays an awareness of modern literature and philosophy, but it remains subservient to Atha's deeply personal concerns. Like Louis Dunkel, Atha is familiar with Freud, but his father is not an Oedipal figure, he is a human being, and Atha retains a love for him, whatever his faults. Moving to London, Atha is surprised at the resentment the (often Communist) students he encounters feel towards their fathers, remembering, 'When I first heard of a young man hating his father, I thought what a very odd thing that was to do, though clearly a certain *chic* attached to it.'[132] He relocates to London in the early thirties, when Marx and Freud dominated student circles, but Atha refuses to consider his father a symbol of political and psychological oppression, preferring to recall how his father has positively shaped his personality. His flirtation with Communism does not represent any deep-seated political conviction (at least none that is explained), but merely serves to engender tension between Atha and his father, the swift diffusion of which heightens Atha's respect for him.

Here, Heppenstall's characterisation was far more conventional, even traditional, and closer to those of his earlier works. Heppenstall also reintroduces his more familiar, poetic descriptive style, abandoning the seemingly colder, 'neutral' style of *The Connecting Door*. In *The Woodshed*, Atha assigned objects emotional significance far more readily, unsurprisingly as they are all implicated in his father's death. Heppenstall often explicates this object meaning, rather than have in it remain in the subtext, as in *The Connecting Door*. Whenever the father's death is directly addressed, this significance tends to be explained at greater length, usually with his signatory idiosyncratic humour. The prospect of a funeral, for example,

---

131   Ibid, p102.

132   Ibid, p104.

prompts amusing reflections: 'The trimmings of death seem unnecessarily tiresome...The State compels one to deal with these dreadful gentlemen in top hats, who are nevertheless left free to organise the matter to their private advantage. Perhaps it was industries like this which Mr Attlee... should have nationalised.'[133]

Although it occasionally name-checks Labour politicians, and is set in a largely proletarian area, *The Woodshed* never claims to be a 'working-class' novel. Indeed, the text's infrequent mentions of class strike the reader as a riposte to those who attempted to determine which modes of writing were appropriate for which social groups. The 'Angry Young Men', who ranged ideologically from moderate left to conservative, attempted to present (neo)-Modernism as fundamentally bourgeois, and irrelevant to proletarian life, implying that their formally reactionary writing was the only literature suitable for the working-classes. Their accusations of 'elitism' levelled at neo-Modernists were underpinned by the assumption that Britain's proletariat were incapable of understanding or enjoying any literature that diverged from traditional forms. This was, of course, ideologically motivated: for them, as for the Socialist Realists, formal experimentation was inherently anarchistic, synonymous with (continental) bourgeois bohemianism, and an opposition to revolutionary politics was implicitly linked to their demand for non-revolutionary literature.

Their novels, unlike Heppenstall's or those of the *école du regard*, contained plenty of 'drama', as traditionally understood. In response, Heppenstall dismissed the apparent connection of class politics with literary form in a sentence: 'Plenty of working-class drama in the family. I suppose we were lower-middle-class.'[134] The proletarian drama that structures their apparently working-class literature becomes the content for a novel written in what was commonly construed as a bourgeois form, populated by

133   Ibid, p30.

134   Ibid, p47.

petit bourgeois characters. Heppenstall's novel deliberately highlights 'its condition as a bourgeois myth' but rather than dwell on class, Atha briefly clarifies his origins, implying that an interest in formal innovation need not be connected to any ideological radicalism, and simply resumes his (at least explicitly) apolitical narrative.[135]

The Woodshed offers the 'pay-off' to which Atha has referred, retaining the aforementioned narrative twist, although this is deliberately written in an immensely anti-climactic fashion. His father dies, as does his aunt, and Atha returns to London by train (mirroring the end of *The Blaze of Noon*). Its 'Coda' is written from the vantage point of 1949, after Atha's final, mysterious Rhineland voyage, when he obsessively notes the changes to his old house, his hometown and his life. He considers, and swiftly rejects, the possibility of returning to Hinderholme, calmly stating, 'Roots. Another dead metaphor. Men are not plants', before concluding that he is 'finished' with the town.[136] The train that takes him away inevitably disappoints, closing his narrative unsatisfactorily, with Atha unable to draw emotional resonance from its mechanistic functions. His melancholic reflection takes one of the *nouveau roman*'s vital theoretical precepts and explicates it at a textual level: 'That was no anthropomorphic cry, no example of the pathetic fallacy. A train whistle is a whistle, blown by steam.'[137]

The 'pay-off' is purely literary: a reflection on the inherently Modernist form that Heppenstall has chosen. 'If consciousness streams, it is backward. Or rather, it is like the slack tide in an estuary...If I again let down the deep trawl of memory, I should bring up dabs and elvers by the ton.'[138] Perhaps Heppenstall felt that the attempts by 'second tradition' writers to capture the workings of the consciousness had inaccurately

---

135 Barthes, *Writing Degree Zero*, p92.

136 *Woodshed*, p132.

137 Ibid, p133.

138 Ibid, p133.

portrayed both the fragmented nature of remembered time and the way it is guided by external objects. Although less radical than the experiments of Joyce and Woolf, Proust and Dujardin, *The Woodshed* remains intriguing, as one of the earliest of many sixties attempts to find new directions for the techniques developed before the war, written in detached, poetic, humorous prose. However, its attempt to escape the 'literary politics' of its form lends it a curiously conciliatory feel, as if Heppenstall stopped short of more radical structural experimentation for fear of offending anti-Modernist sensibilities.

It was primarily *The Connecting Door*, then, which made sixties critics mark Rayner Heppenstall as an 'experimental' novelist. Cixous praised *The Connecting Door*, detailing how '*l'auteur abolit la différence entre les temps de réflexion et les âges du sujet avec un sens dramatique de l'humour*'.[139] Anthony Burgess also reviewed it favourably. It shared many traits with the *nouveau roman*: Randall Stevenson was one of several English critics to retroactively identify it as one of Britain's most successful attempts to engage with the French development, explaining how, 'In the manner of Robbe-Grillet, [*Connecting Door*] remains a puzzle, raising and frustrating the possibility of creating a plausible pattern for its events...offering only a series of 'connecting doors' into irreconcilable planes of time or reality.'[140]

It is intriguing that this teasing of the reader escaped Julian Symons, who offered many perceptive insights on *Saturnine*. Symons felt that *The Connecting Door*'s relentless description of actualities 'quickly becomes tedious' and that there was 'little of the delight in playing games with himself and with the reader that runs through Robbe-Grillet's work' or of the French novelist's determination 'to leave everything uncertain'. It is strange that Symons should so completely deny *The Connecting Door*'s tex-

---

139   Cixous, p16.

140   Randall Stevenson, *The British Novel since the Thirties* (B. T. Batsford: London 1986), p213.

tual play: Heppenstall's structural experimentation remains forefronted (and captivating) throughout, although perhaps, in abandoning his usual prose style, Heppenstall was not writing to his lyrical strengths.[141] Nevertheless, *The Connecting Door* remains more studied than any Heppenstall novel besides *The Blaze of Noon*: whereas his earlier novel anticipated the *nouveau roman*, *The Connecting Door*, in its attempt to narrow the gap between post-war English and French literature, often seemed an attempt to simply mimic the products of its late fifties heyday, reflected in the Heppenstall's clearly discernable shift of structural and textual style to one closer to Robbe-Grillet's.

The Woodshed, however, attempted to connect Britain's burgeoning neo-Modernist literature to pre-war 'high' Modernism: it was perhaps more typical of its time and place, with Burgess (in *A Clockwork Orange*), Johnson (in *Trawl*) and Quin (in *Berg*) all attempting to pick up where they felt Joyce and company had left off. Their prose, perhaps, was more polemically radical: while the fiercely 'experimental' *Connecting Door* provoked substantial critical interest, *The Woodshed*, striking the casual reader as a modest, unambitious work, barely received any. Even Symons ignored it, perhaps because, for all the refined qualities of Heppenstall's prose, its refusal of any deeper meaning than made textually explicit negated any real sense of the novel's *necessity* – it reads pleasantly but does not demand as much further consideration as Heppenstall's previous novels. Unlike *The Connecting Door*, its ending leaves nothing unresolved; although it engages with its own form humorously and intelligently, and by no means lacks literary merit, *The Woodshed* fails to conduct an investigation into its own structure or the position of the individual within a specific historical moment that stands up to deep analysis as do *The Blaze of Noon*, *Saturnine* or *The Connecting Door*.

It is *The Connecting Door* that fascinates more consistently, as an 'ex-

---

141   Symons, p20.

perimental' British attempt at an 'anti-novel' and in its own right: sympathetic critics hoped that Heppenstall's creative renaissance would produce several more neo-Modernist works constructed along similar lines. However, Heppenstall followed this path no further, and when he finally issued another novel, it assumed an entirely different form.

One Memory, One Oblivion:
The Absent Legacy of Rayner Heppenstall

'I, as an experimental father figure, am out of touch with my juniors...[who] believe in a sort of progress in the novel, their sort of novel superseding the traditional novel, as socialism...supersedes capitalism.'[142]

Characteristically shifting his focus, Heppenstall never attempted another 'anti-novel'. However, he maintained his productivity rate throughout the sixties. He published translations of Châteaubriand's *Atala* and *René*, and two volumes of memoirs, *The Intellectual Part* and *A Portrait of the Artist as a Professional Man*. His monograph, *Raymond Roussel: A Critical Guide* (1966) was complemented by a co-translation of Roussel's *Impressions d'Afrique* with his daughter Lindy Foord. He also issued another novel, *The Shearers*. *A Little Pattern of French Crime* accompanied it, both indicating a surprising change of direction: his dominant interest was now criminology.

Heppenstall also shifted ideologically. Previously, he had refrained from declaring any sympathies: he did so in 1963, lamenting that he had adopted 'distinctly right-wing political attitudes', adding, 'I have not enjoyed this drift to the Right. I hope it will be reversed.'[143] It was not. Discussing Roussel, Heppenstall stated, 'I do not myself subscribe to... revolutionary optimism, either politically or aesthetically...progressivism gone wrong is now a pervasive nuisance.'[144] Heppenstall criticised

---

142   Goodman, p71.

143   *Intellectual Part*, p218.

144   Heppenstall, *Raymond Roussel: A Critical Guide* (Calder & Boyars: London 1966), p90.

Foucault and Robbe-Grillet's writings on Roussel; he also mentioned that the term 'anti-novel' originated in 1627, with Charles Sorel's *Le Berger Extravagant, ou l'Anti-roman*, suggesting that 'in significant literary history, the anti-novel preceded the novel', by which he meant the post-Enlightenment, nineteenth-century novel.[145] Here, Heppenstall still displayed an interest in the *nouveau roman*: he never again discussed it in a book, and later translated Balzac's *Splendeurs et Misères des Courtisanes*, despite Robbe-Grillet deploring the fact that 'The only conception of the novel to have currency today is...that of Balzac.'[146]

In 1969, Heppenstall published *A Portrait of the Artist as a Professional Man*, about his time at the BBC, alongside his book on French crime and *The Shearers*. This concerned the murder trial of eight members of the Shearer family, several conceived incestuously. Re-adopting his more familiar lyrical prose style, which contrasted markedly with the coarse dialect of its protagonists, *The Shearers* was unique among Heppenstall's novels in that it was written almost entirely in the third person, very briefly adopting the first person perspective of a family member. A film company purchased the rights to the novel, but never acted upon them; that his novel was considered filmable was also unusual.[147] *The Shearers* produced little narrative tension, with the reader never doubting its outcome. Rather, it attempted, with limited success, to explore the family's twisted psychologies and to study the effects of heightened media interest upon them and their trial. Heppenstall interspersed his narrative with contemporary events, attempting to simultaneously present the trial as a microcosm of civilisation, and civilisation as coldly indifferent. After its conclusion, its final paragraph laments: 'in the end, they will all fall, even the moon. Meanwhile, aeroplanes crash,

---

145   Ibid, p92.

146   Robbe-Grillet, 'A Future for the Novel', p15. Heppenstall's translation was entitled *A Harlot High and Low* (1970).

147   Goodman, p47.

tall buildings collapse, and the world's sleepers lie pinned to their beds. The earth turns.'[148]

During the seventies, Heppenstall issued four more criminological works, not publishing another novel until *Two Moons* (1977). He had been somewhat typecast by his inclusion in B. S. Johnson's list of praiseworthy novelists, which included 'Samuel Beckett (of course), John Berger, Christine Brooke-Rose, Brigid Brophy, Anthony Burgess, Alan Burns, Angela Carter, Eva Figes, Giles Gordon, Wilson Harris, Rayner Heppenstall, even hasty, muddled Robert Nye, Ann Quin, Penelope Shuttle, Alan Sillitoe (for his last book only, *Raw Material* indeed), Stefan Themerson and (coming) John Wheway.'[149] His relationship with Johnson's circle had been fractious: he disliked their tendency to link political and formal radicalism, and disdained 'experimentalism which has recourse to typographical oddity.'[150] By 1977, Johnson and Quin had committed suicide, and their loosely constituted circle had collapsed, but *Two Moons* relied upon the very 'typographical oddity' Heppenstall had previously claimed to despise.

The Shearers, despite its disturbing subject matter, retained Heppenstall's poetic prose style and only occasionally suggested his autumnal political attitudes, keeping external details subservient to its plot. *Two Moons* did the opposite. Dominated by impenetrable astrological rhetoric, it was autobiographical, about Heppenstall/Atha's son becoming paralysed. It comprised two narratives, running consecutively on its left and right-hand pages, which Heppenstall rather tediously explained during its right-hand story. However, the left-hand narrative ended where the right-hand one began, rendering this crude device pointless as the reader could simply disregard it and read them sequentially, rather than simultaneously.

Moreover, Harold Atha's story is overwhelmed by endless arbitrary

---

148 Heppenstall, *The Shearers* (Hamish Hamilton: London 1969), p199.

149 Johnson, pp29-30.

150 Goodman, p67n.

details, such as 'Norwich confirmed their First Division quality by taking Arsenal in their stride.'[151] These exterior details lacked the considered intellectualisation that made Heppenstall's earlier prose so captivating, despite occasionally amusing (but often, as when he details the suicides of Quin and Johnson, morbid) metafictional references to Atha's literary career, obviously Heppenstall's. They obsessively contemplate death, and while the author rarely passes explicit political comment, their very selection – often concerning crime, immigration, the Welfare State and strikes implies strong right-wing sympathies.

Julian Symons considered *Two Moons* an 'unhappy case of French flu', criticising the underlying structural simplicity of its apparently innovative formalisation.[152] Heppenstall privately complained about contemporary reviews: Ronald Harwood 'says nothing whatever about the content, but simply makes clever remarks about the form' while to Lorna Sage, 'I am mad'.[153] Retrospectively, their engagement purely with its form seems a kindness. Both the form *and* content of *Two Moons* reduced John Carey to apoplexy: Carey, incensed by Heppenstall's use of newspaper headlines to frame his personal narrative, which to Carey was nothing more considered than a snobbish barb at 'the masses,' claimed, 'The avant-garde technique of the novel excludes ordinary readers' – preposterously, seeing as Heppenstall explicitly stated that his simple technique could be ignored – and accused him of appropriating 'his son's hurt,' as if Heppenstall had not been genuinely affected by it.[154]

Two Moons was clearly the work of someone suffering from severe depression – specifically, the familiar world-weariness of a tired, disillusioned Englishman (and former Socialist) drifting further and further to

---

151   Heppenstall, *Two Moons* (Allison & Busby: London 1977), p103.

152   Symons, p20.

153   Goodman, p219.

154   Carey, p211.

the Right, hardly unusual for a man of Heppenstall's background and age in late seventies Britain. If *Two Moons* was ideologically problematic, then *The Pier* was irreconcilable. The novel is ostensibly about old age, concerning an elderly writer's detestation for his neighbours, but fundamentally, it is about death. Harold Atha plans a novel about these neighbours: he is assailed by numerous health problems, ranging from toothache to a stroke. His concerns are those of an elderly bourgeois – much is made, for example, of Atha's irritation at having to return footballs to the neighbouring children. Atha is highly conservative in his dotage: he reads *The Daily Mail*, and considers Margaret Thatcher 'admirable'.[155] Finally, he murders most of his neighbours, framing one of them. Written as a diary, *The Pier* is, generally, formally unremarkable. It is metafictional, but lacks any real imagination or innovation. Its conclusion is deeply unsatisfying: the characterisation of Atha and his neighbours is not sufficient to earn sympathy for the final action of the protagonist, which is frustratingly predictable.

Many passages in *The Pier* were directly reproduced from Heppenstall's journals, edited by fellow criminologist Jonathan Goodman and simultaneously published in 1986. Covering 1969 to 1981 (Heppenstall destroyed his journals written prior to 1969, denying these later writings a wider context), they offered only occasional insights into Rayner's literary career, providing instead a distressing insight into his severe depression, filled with distressing passages outlining his (unrealised) plans to commit suicide, diatribes against strikes, Arabs, blacks, the Irish and over-population, and inconsequential reflections such as 'I was a Socialist then.'[156] Published posthumously, but before Heppenstall had completely faded from cultural memory, they often make difficult reading from a contemporary vantagepoint. While, admittedly, they contain little that Heppenstall did not at least hint at elsewhere, they appeared when the author was no longer alive

---

155 Heppenstall, *The Pier* (Allison & Busby: London 1986), p58.

156 Goodman, p198.

to explain or defend himself, and they have occasionally provided am-
munition for Heppenstall's personal critics.

* * *

Writing the first English monograph, Heppenstall complained of the
'critical vacuum' around Roussel – that vacuum has been filled, largely
thanks to his work on the Frenchman, but no critical study of Heppenstall
has ever been published.[157] Neither has a biography: Johnson's reputation
has recently been reinvigorated by Jonathan Coe's magnificent *Like a
Fiery Elephant*, which reminded critics of his prominence within sixties
neo-Modernism (and of neo-Modernism), while Roger Lewis' obsessively
vitriolic study of Anthony Burgess moved critics to attack the biographer
more than to negatively reassess his subject. Unlike Burgess and Johnson,
none of Heppenstall's novels were ever filmed. Given their knowing use
of anti-cinematic prose, they would represent a fascinating challenge to an
adventurous director, but their obscurity means that, unlike several other
apparently 'un-filmable' novels, the challenge remains unmet.

European critics often assessed Heppenstall more favourably, but few
had any continuing interest in preserving his memory. To them, he was
a talented writer, whose engagement with French literature contrasted
agreeably with the parochialism of some English novelists, but they had
other concerns. They believed that, however cosmopolitan, Heppenstall
was an English author who should be considered within his national context, and left the determination of his standing to the British.

It was Britain's anti-Modernists who were allowed to shape the (non-)
memory of Rayner Heppenstall, and deprived of any domestic reputation,
his international standing has suffered proportionately. Rayner's journals
were named 'The Master Eccentric' after C. P. Snow's characterisation

---

157   *Raymond Roussel*, p88.

of him. For aesthetic conservatives like Carey, hoping to promote the contemporaneous 'traditional' novels of Arnold Bennett and others as a counterpoint to 'elitist' Modernism, the furiously conservative statements contained in Heppenstall's journals and final novels could easily be co-opted into a critique of Modernist and neo-Modernist political attitudes.

Throughout his lifetime, Heppenstall made plenty of enemies. Some, including Evelyn Waugh, publicly stated their dislike for him.[158] Heppenstall's honest, often self-effacing memoirs made no attempt to hide or justify any of the more problematic aspects of his character. Consequently, in Britain, he has been judged far more on his perceived personality, and all but banished from cultural memory. By his autumnal years, nobody (except Julian Symons, with reservations) seemed prepared to defend him on formal terms: he had outlived Johnson, his most passionate English advocate, while Cixous discussed him no further, and the French 'anti-novelists' produced nothing significant on his work.

Perhaps British formalists were dismayed at his failure to become a domestic equivalent to Robbe-Grillet. After such a long wait, the re-alisation (with *The Shearers*) that Heppenstall had abandoned the *nouveau roman* was inevitably disappointing, and *Two Moons* confirmed to them that Heppenstall had become an anachronism. They might have been prepared to ignore his politics if his post-1962 novels had not failed so completely in their attempted experimentation with form. Heppenstall's fiction had always placed itself outside any ideological consensus, but previously, this individualism had seemed enigmatic and challenging, and had been allied to genuinely interesting literary constructions. To cite just one example, Eliot (Heppenstall's defining poetic influence) continued to produce inventive, rewarding work after publicly declaring his arch conservatism, and critics continued to consider his work on its aesthetic merits, rather than focusing primarily on his ideological position. Heppenstall did not, but it is surprising that his earlier works whose magic lies not just in their

---

158   Goodman, pp238-242.

formal innovation but also their intangible ideology and intoxicating exploration of alternative belief systems have also been forgotten after being derided by anti-formalist critics since he published *Two Moons*.

Maybe, too, he explained the method behind *The Connecting Door* (as Robbe-Grillet explained his methods in various critical articles, and Roussel explained his in *How I Wrote Certain of My Works*) too definitively and too soon in *The Intellectual Part*, undermining its mystique under a year after its publication. That is not to discredit *The Intellectual Part*, the most consistently interesting volume of Heppenstall's memoirs, but his lengthy explication of the process of creating 'an extra grammatical tense' to 'set up a new, implicit time-dimension' dispelled all ambiguity about the novel's temporality, the resolution of which constituted its challenge to the reader.[159]

Ultimately, Heppenstall failed to disentangle 'the confusion of aesthetics with politics'; unsurprisingly, given how many literati and politicians had vested interests in upholding entrenched, ideologically expedient concepts of formal semiotics.[160] The neo-Modernists, like the *nouveau romanciers*, were principally interested in formal innovation. The reactionaries opposing them dismissed the *nouveau roman* as a foreign development, and managed to successfully portray the domestic attempt to rehabilitate Modernism as a failure, using the suicides of Quin and (particularly) Johnson as evidence.

British neo-Modernism never approached the critical status of the *nouveau roman*, and the works of the '*école du regard*' shared far more characteristics than those of England's 'experimental' circle, who simply shared an attitude. Johnson's attempts to unify such a disparate group of writers, linked only by an (often reserved) opposition to 'traditional' literature, were rather contrived, and those listed authors who attracted the most critical interest (Burgess, Angela Carter, Sillitoe) were not those who

---

159   *Intellectual Part*, p214.

160   Goodman, p71.

attended Johnson's *avant-garde* soirees. Whilst some authors associated with this project have achieved certain success when judged individually, particularly Carter, whose incisive explorations of gender roles have made her one of her country's most studied novelists, the wider attempt to construct a *nouveau roman*-style 'movement' (one similar in intention if not in style) has, for many years, been excluded from British literary history.

Neo-Modernism was swiftly superseded by post-Modernism, a critical framework through which the novels of Carter (and, occasionally, Johnson) have often been read. Neo-Modernism was an important precursor, especially if the *nouveau roman* is considered as French neo-Modernism. It prompted the continuation of the discourse of Modernist writing, facilitating the strand of post-Modernism that extended Modernism's key investigations, rather than distancing itself from them. Those who realised this less successfully, simply reviving Modernist techniques after they had ceased to be formally revolutionary, inevitably did not make the same impact as the *nouveau roman* authors.

Mainly, Johnson's associates failed to make a decisive intervention into western literary culture, operating after the *nouveau roman* had achieved their aim of reviving and reinvigorating the Modernist project. But Heppenstall was an anomaly: two decades older than Johnson, he had personally experienced the dissolution of Modernism amidst the demand for heightened political concentration and the implication of many Modernist personalities in ideological atrocities. Seen by the neo-Modernists as the British representative of the *nouveau roman*, Johnson sent Heppenstall his first novel asking if it 'had anything in common with the new French novel. It didn't.'[161] Ultimately, he was a forefather to Johnson's neo-Modernist circle, not an active participant, having already produced several novels that *did* take 'bourgeois' Modernism in new, original directions.

The critical consensus – of Bowen, Cixous, Stevenson and the 'Italian

---

161   Ibid, p67*n*.

critic' – was that *The Blaze of Noon* did this most successfully. It was re-printed several times, in 1940, 1962, 1968 and 1980: *The Connecting Door* and *The Woodshed* were reissued once (in 1968), perhaps because of their affinities with the works of other neo-Modernists published by Calder and Boyars. Despite its occasional reappearances (and translations into French, German and Italian), *The Blaze of Noon* remains no more than a footnote to thirties literature. Its initial characterisation as literary pornography meant that it caused an minor sensation: once this faded, the novel was lost amidst its war-time circumstances, and the attempts of Cixous and the Arts Council to raise awareness of it failed.

As we have seen, *The Blaze of Noon* has nearly always been judged in relation to the *nouveau roman*, just as *The Woodshed* has been assessed in the context of British neo-Modernism, with *The Connecting Door* straddling the two. To judge Heppenstall's earlier novels in relation to the *nouveau roman* makes more sense, especially given his far greater enthusiasm for it. Like the *école du regard*, his novels prioritised structural organisation and metafictional awareness above incendiary prose stylisation, something that distinguished him from many British (neo-)Modernists, who mostly operated within Britain's 'second tradition'.

But whilst the *école du regard*'s loosely constituted principles, and their practical explorations of those principles, provide an interesting framework within which to criticise Heppenstall, it would be unfair not to judge him within the wider context of (late) Modernist writing, and, most importantly, on his own considerable literary merits. Each novel, too, should be judged individually. His output was extraordinarily varied, ranging from the unclassifiable *Blaze of Noon* to the dual-narrative *Two Moons*, encompassing Britain's most compelling 'anti-novel', an amiable 'stream-of-consciousness' work, a spectacularly inventive revival of the *picaresque* form and a similarly unique war novel. A genuinely eclectic range of influences coloured his fiction, which explains why his aesthetic position shifted so frequently and so radically. Heppenstall displayed an astonishingly broad knowledge of literary and intellectual history, in his novels, his memoirs, and his criticism that, even if it lacked the theoretical rigour of some of his contemporaries, is consistently peppered with amusing diversions, bold (and often bizarre) opinions and moments of startling perception.

Heppenstall's novels (and other writings) were aesthetically unified by his immediately recognisable prose, whose style can be located within the context of a literary discourse that ran from French Symbolism to the *nouveau roman*, but, at its best, was delightfully original. Thematically, they all explored the position of the individual (usually a cultured bourgeois, like Heppenstall) within a complex, hostile or indifferent modernity. There was always an underlying skepticism about the feasibility of imposing any overarching political or philosophical system — all types of 'plot' — upon it.[162] This arose from his belief that any dreams of collectively improving 'the world' ignored the fact that the modern individual lived in a state of acute isolation, which is conveyed particularly strongly in *The Blaze of Noon* and *The Lesser Infortune*.

Digressing briefly, his BBC radio commissions were equally eclectic, comprising attempts to bring interesting domestic and European authors to public attention, adaptations of writers from Shakespeare to Orwell, and various original scripts. If these ever became widely accessible (only *The Fool's Saga*, an adaptation of the story on which Shakespeare based *Hamlet*, was ever published), Heppenstall's engagement with this inherently modern form of broadcasting could also be understood, alongside his literary output. As it stands, his radio projects have become as obscure (if not *more* obscure) as his fiction. Heppenstall complained that they curtailed his literary productivity, but perhaps they are also worthy of reappraisal, although nothing is likely to become available unless his novels achieve a significantly higher critical standing.

---

162 *Double Image*, p73.

Heppenstall's novels provide a different way of considering the relationship between form and content. Often conceptually separated, in Heppenstall's novels, they could never be fully extricated. Heppenstall never, except in *Two Moons*, constructed his narrative according to a given formal-theoretical precept; rather, the content determined which forms he created, meaning they were seamlessly integrated.

'If there was derivation, it was devious or even merely *zeitgeistig*.'[163] So wrote Rayner Heppenstall in response to the Italian critic who dubbed him 'the founder of the *nouveau roman*'. Heppenstall would, however, have doubtlessly agreed that he should not determine how he is remembered, any more than Carey, Cixous or anyone else. Symons concluded that, 'as a whole [Heppenstall], having perhaps been over-valued in the sixties…is certainly underrated today.'[164] Nothing has changed. There *is* a British canon to which authors are admitted solely on the basis of the perceived originality of their formal experimentation, but Heppenstall, for whatever reasons, has been excluded, despite having been repeatedly credited with initiating an important development within European counter-traditional literature.

The possibility of his acceptance, assuming that the British neo-Modernist authors will continue to be assessed individually in the absence of a 'movement' that achieved a similar validity to its French predecessor, most likely rests on one question. Did he found the *nouveau roman*? Aptly, there is no definitive conclusion. To begin the process of Heppenstall's rehabilitation, it is probably best to suggest he did, and there are enough structural and textual similarities between *The Blaze of Noon*, *Saturnine* and *The Lesser Infortune* and the works of the *école du regard* to justify such an assertion. Whether or not those novelists were directly inspired by *The*

---

163   *Intellectual Part*, p212.

164   Symons, p20.

Blaze of Noon is secondary: Heppenstall's novels guided Modernist sensibilities into his own original direction, thus making them successful on their own terms.

However, nothing can appropriately be argued about Heppenstall without a degree of ambivalence, and we should also consider that *Saturnine* and *The Lesser Infortune* were conceived (like *The Woodshed*, and, ironically, *The Connecting Door*) as reflexive, distinctive contributions to an existing genre, not as works that would initiate a new one. Even if he later argued that if any of his novels anticipated the *nouveau roman*, it was *The Lesser Infortune*, unfortunately not published until that 'movement' had already begun to register with the French critical consciousness. He would also have argued, rightly, that whether or not he did so was not the primary issue. Heppenstall's novels were poetic, considered and intelligently realised engagements with literary form, and, regardless of the sub-discourses of Modernist writing they can justifiably be situated within, they deserve a far better reputation.

Bibliography

Works by Rayner Heppenstall

Novels

The Blaze of Noon (Sphere: London 1967).

The Connecting Door (Barrie & Rockliff: London 1962).

The Greater Infortune (Peter Owen: London 1960).

The Lesser Infortune (Jonathan Cape: London 1953).

The Pier (Allison & Busby: London 1986).

Saturnine (Secker & Warburg: London 1943).

The Shearers (Hamish Hamilton: London 1969).

Two Moons (Allison & Busby: London 1977).

The Woodshed (Calder & Boyars: London 1968).

Criticism

The Double Image (Secker & Warburg: London 1947).

The Fourfold Tradition: Notes on English and French Literatures, with Some Ethnological and Historical Asides (Barrie & Rockliff: London 1961).

'Petron' in *The Criterion* Vol. XV (1935), pp333-335.

Raymond Roussel: A Critical Guide (Calder & Boyars: London 1966).

Memoirs

Four Absentees (Cardinal: London 1988).

The Intellectual Part (Barrie & Rockliff: London 1963).

Poetry

'Mary of Magdala' in *Poems 1933-1945* (Martin Secker & Warburg: London 1946), pp92-93.

'Uneasy Time' in *Poems 1933-45*, p11.

Other Works

Roland Barthes, *The Pleasure of the Text* (Jonathan Cape: London 1975).

Roland Barthes, *Writing Degree Zero* (Jonathan Cape: London 1967).

Celia Britton, *The Nouveau Roman: Fiction, Theory and Politics* (MacMillan: London & Basingstoke 1992).

John Carey, *The Intellectuals and the Masses: Pride and Prejudice among the Literary Intelligentsia, 1888-1939* (Faber & Faber: London 1992).

Hélène Cixous, 'Langage et regard dans le roman experiméntal: Grand-Bretagne' in *Le Monde*, 6959.viia. (18 May 1967), p16.

Paul de Man, 'The Rhetoric of Blindness: Jacques Derrida's Reading of Rousseau' in *Blindness and Insight: Essays in the Rhetoric of Contemporary Criticism* (Routledge: London 1986), pp102-141.

Jacques Derrida, 'Force and Signification' in *Writing and Difference* (Routledge: London 2003), pp1-35.

Jacques Derrida, 'The Law of Genre' in *Acts of Literature* (Routledge: New York/London 1992), pp221-252.

Jonathan Goodman (ed.), *The Master Eccentric: The Journals of Rayner Heppenstall 1969-1981* (Allison & Busby: London 1986).

Stephen Heath, *The Nouveau Roman* (Elek: London 1972), p30.

B. S. Johnson, *Aren't You Rather Young to be Writing Your Memoirs?* (Hutchinson: London 1973).

Alain Robbe-Grillet, 'A Future for the Novel' in *For a New Novel: Essays on Fiction* (Grove Press: New York 1965), pp15-24.

Alain Robbe-Grillet, 'New Novel, New Man' in *For a New Novel*, pp133-142.

Alain Robbe-Grillet, 'On Several Obsolete Notions' in *For a New Novel*, pp25-48.

Alain Robbe-Grillet, 'The Use of Theory' in *For a New Novel*, pp7-14.

Nathalie Sarraute, 'The Age of Suspicion' in *Tropisms and The Age of Suspicion* (John Calder: London 1963).

Jean-Paul Sartre, *What is Literature?* (Harper & Row: New York 1965).

Randall Stevenson, *The British Novel Since the Thirties: An Introduction* (B. T. Batsford: London 1987).

John Sturrock, *The French New Novel: Claude Simon, Michel Butor, Alain Robbe-Grillet* (OUP: Oxford 1969).

Julian Symons, 'Beyond Everyday Life' in *The London Review of Books*, Volume III, Issue 4 (5-19 March 1981), pp19-20.

SELECTED DALKEY ARCHIVE PAPERBACKS

FOR A FULL LIST OF PUBLICATIONS, VISIT:
www.dalkeyarchive.com

SELECTED DALKEY ARCHIVE PAPERBACKS